STAR TREK
THE NEXT GENERATION®

MAXIMUM WARP

BOOK ONE OF TWO

Dave Galanter and Greg Brodeur
Based upon STAR TREK and
STAR TREK: THE NEXT GENERATION
created by Gene Roddenberry.

POCKET BOOKS
New York   London   Toronto   Sydney   Singapore

An *Original* Publication of POCKET BOOKS

POCKET BOOKS, a division of Simon & Schuster, Inc.
1230 Avenue of the Americas, New York, NY 10020

Copyright © 2001 by Paramount Pictures. All Rights Reserved.

A VIACOM COMPANY

STAR TREK is a Registered Trademark of
Paramount Pictures.

This book is published by Pocket Books, a division of
Simon & Schuster, Inc., under exclusive license from
Paramount Pictures.

ISBN: 0-671-04749-3

First Pocket Books printing March 2001

10 9 8 7 6 5 4 3 2 1

POCKET and colophon are registered trademarks of
Simon & Schuster, Inc.

Printed in the U.S.A.

"You accepted the *Enterprise's* proposition more rapidly than I expected."

J'emery smiled. "Yes, I did. But Picard is too gullible to see that. We have enough power for disruptors?"

Folan nodded, her superior's treachery now clear. "Yes, Commander. Two short bursts."

"Excellent. One for Picard's shuttle, another for *Enterprise* herself. And they are without shields. . . ." His eyes a bit gleeful, J'emery pounded his fist lightly on the arm of his command chair. "With Picard gone, and the *Enterprise* further disabled, the Praetor will have a nice prize when we return home."

"If I may, Commander," Folan said. "This is directly against current Senate policy with regard to Federation vessels. As well, I believe the *Enterprise* is truly offering a means of escape for us both. I've gone over their data—"

"Science is your strength, Folan, but tactics are not. You are as gullible as Picard."

Folan pursed her lips and stifled a retort that would not serve her well. "How else might we restore our powerless systems?"

"Even without communications from us, we will be missed. In a day, at the most, a ship will be searching for us."

"I fear life support will not last that long, Commander. Especially if we divert battery power to the weapons array."

J'emery turned directly toward her as he rose from his seat. "You have your orders, Folan. When Picard is halfway here, destroy his shuttle."

BOOK ONE

DEAD ZONE

The glories of our blood and state
Are shadows, not substantial things;
There is no armour against fate;
Death lays his icy hands on kings.

—JAMES SHIRLEY

Chapter One

U.S.S. Enterprise, NCC-1701-E
Romulan Neutral Zone
Section 19

Three weeks ago

"TRANSFER AUXILIARY POWER to shields. I want those sensors on-line. What's happened to main power?"

"I don't know, sir. Warp and impulse are off-line. Helm is not responding."

"Thrusters to station-keeping." Captain Jean-Luc Picard jabbed at the panel on the arm of his command chair. "Picard to Engineering. What's happening down there?"

Silence.

"Comm systems are down, Captain." Lieutenant Chamberlain's voice from tactical was tense but con-

3

trolled. "Aux power is not responding, sir. Life support is on battery backup and holding."

Picard spun toward the ensign at the engineering station. "Get down there, Bradley. Have Mr. Riker return with a report on all systems, and have Engineering put priority on sensors and shields."

Bounding from his chair and into the turbolift, Bradley only had time for a half-nod and a chopped, "Aye, sir."

The captain hoped he had put priority on the right systems. Eyes and claws—it seemed logical. But without knowing the status of Engineering . . . He half wanted to race down there himself. "Helm?" He edged toward the conn.

Ensign Barbara Rossi shook her head. "Still negative helm control, sir, but thrusters *are* maintaining station-keeping." Only her second month on bridge duty, Picard thought, and she was suddenly steering an anchor, not a starship.

The captain leaned over the helm and ran his own hands over the near-dead controls. No helm, no sensors, and the last reading they *did* get was of a Romulan warbird decloaking between them and the Federation cargo hauler that had found itself stuck in the Neutral Zone.

It wasn't long before the starboard lift door opened, and Picard pivoted toward it as Commander William Riker shot onto the bridge.

"Status?" Picard demanded.

Riker dropped down to the lower deck. "Verified we've lost all main power. Sickbay is on internal batteries. So are the lifts. Every nonessential system is down." He lowered himself into the console seat at Picard's right. "Inertial dampers and SIF generators are using the artificial gravity power grid. La Forge did that first."

"Repair estimate?"

"None, yet. We don't even know why it's happened."

"Not good enough," Picard said. "We need the cause. Romulan defensive weapon? Sabotage?"

"I thought we were supposed to be allies now."

The captain grunted. "Supposed to be" was the key phrase. The Dominion War was over finally, at great cost. Now some allies, in their weakness, could turn paranoid toward their war-weary partners.

Riker shook his head, and a single strand of dark hair bounced once before becoming matted to his damp forehead. "Well, whatever it is, it's the damnedest thing I've ever seen, sir. Everything but electrical power seems dead. Even Data is having problems. He's had to switch around all his internal power settings."

Picard looked up, then rose, taking a step toward . . . he wasn't sure where. "Data? How bad?"

"Not sure. He said he'll 'function adequately' for now. I'm guessing that's the android equivalent of a stiff upper lip. But if whatever's keeping us from using most of our power systems is hampering him, too, that tells me it's not internal to our systems." Riker's tone was suddenly softer, more concerned. "He's working through it. He wants to deploy an optic buoy so we can see what's going on outside." He shook his head. "Blasted bay doors won't override manually. I'm not even sure they've found the old buoy. Pretty old technology."

Turning toward the blank forward viewscreen, Picard glared, wishing he could see right through the bulkhead. "Let's assume this is some dampening field the Romulans have developed as a defensive tool." That would have been a better assumption before the Dominion War. Now . . . would the peace fall apart so quickly? There was no way to know. A Romulan ship with a renegade commander could be mistrustful of the *Enterprise* appearing in the Neutral Zone. Picard might have been, if the situation were reversed, and he was no renegade. Usually.

The captain turned back to Riker. "Signal General Quarters, deck by deck. Until the internal comms are working, we fall back on relays. Then see if hand phasers are working. Priorities: arming the crew, sensors, shields, communications. Go."

"On screen." Picard usually didn't have to wait so long for such a simple order to be followed, but in the moments that dragged on into minutes, he did just that. He paced a bit, not wanting to sit down. Any moment he thought he'd hear the hum and feel the static of a Romulan transporter beam. An enemy guard could be deposited next to him, behind him . . . throughout his ship. He held a phaser in his hand, ready. It was useless, he'd learned just moments earlier. Fully charged phasers, not working.

The trigger was warm to the touch. Hand phasers worked on battery packs, so why didn't they work when they should have? And why did he still keep it in his hand, now that he knew it was a dunsel? What would he do? Throw it at a Romulan invader? The idea that the Romulans would offer resistance rather than help was probably wrong, in any case. There had been good relations with the Romulans since the end of the war. But he couldn't get the feeling out of the back of his mind that something was just . . . entirely wrong here.

Again, a bit too harshly, he ordered, "Visual tie in, Ensign Rossi."

"Trying, sir."

Of course—it wasn't his crew's fault. Optical buoys were low-tech and hard to calibrate. But they ran on battery power, and they didn't broadcast in subspace. With one deployed, *Enterprise* would at least have eyes outside the ship. And ears—they might be able to set up local-space communications as well. He'd have preferred that shields and sensors came on-line first . . . but he'd take what he could get. "Ensign Shapiro?"

"Still nothing, sir." The ops officer shook his head. He struggled with the old-fashioned, seldom-used comm protocols, not something heavily taught at the Academy. "Coming through now, Captain."

Static-scratched and jumpy, a picture formed on the main viewscreen. Space looked odd, black. A digital picture, not one created by sensors. Digital. Video. Antique.

But even with the electronic equivalent of naked eyes, a Romulan warbird's stalking presence was unmistakable in the distance.

Picard moved toward the viewer, standing between Rossi at the conn and Shapiro at ops. "Try to raise them, and the cargo ship as well."

"Aye, sir."

Shapiro toiled again with his mostly lifeless console.

"Cargo ship doesn't respond, Captain. They may not be able to read a frequency this low. Visual data only . . . they appear to be drifting. No external lights or beacons."

A nod, and Picard paced a step away. He thumbed his chin thoughtfully. "And the Romulans?"

"No response yet. But they should be able to hear us if they're monitoring these bandwidths."

"If they're smart, they're monitoring all bandwidths," Picard murmured.

Suddenly, Shapiro looked up, slightly surprised. "Captain, they're returning the hail."

"Hold a moment." He turned toward the rear of the bridge and holstered his phaser. "Voices low. Let's not show all our cards. As far as this ship is concerned, we're doing as well as we can sell them." He turned back to Shapiro. "Now, patch them through."

"Patch" was right. Picard had time to pace between the helm and the command chair three times before he settled into his seat. Finally, the warbird commander appeared on the viewer.

No need for introductions. They knew who commanded the *Enterprise.* And Picard knew the Romulan by appearance as well.

"Commander . . . J'emery, is it?"

The Romulan's features were marked with distaste, dark angles cutting in on themselves. His upswept brows were creased with tension. "Testing some new weapon, Picard? I'd accuse you of treachery, but perhaps foolhardiness is the word. *If* treaty violations were the only matter at hand. But acts of war . . ."

Ofttimes Picard had found the will to play this game, but not today. Not sitting in the middle of the Neutral Zone, dead in space. It was interesting that J'emery hadn't mentioned why it had taken them a bit to hail the Romulans. Interesting indeed. Picard looked intently at J'emery, and wished he could glance around the Romulan bridge as well. "You know, Commander, I think we'll just bypass the chess match this time. You know why we're here, and you know that the treaty allows us a certain leeway for rescue missions. You're supposed to offer assistance."

Seeming to gather more of his composure, perhaps strengthened by the game Picard didn't wish to play, J'emery straightened, grew cocky. "I don't like this new treaty, Picard. I suppose you'd allow me to rescue a stray battle group that wandered off course and found itself in Earth's orbit?"

Picard pressed his lips into a thin line. "We can work with each other, or against each other, Commander. Which do you think will end this situation satisfactorily for us both?"

J'emery faltered a moment, looking at someone offscreen. "I'll—" For a moment, the Romulan seemed to rise from his chair oddly, almost as if levitating. "We'll consider that," the Romulan said hastily, and the screen went blank.

Twisting her head toward her captain, Rossi's brows knitted in a quizzical look. "They cut the feed."

"Was he . . ." Picard hesitated. "Did they just lose gravity?"

* * *

"What in the Praetor's name is going on?" Commander J'emery meant to be as severe as possible, Sub-Commander Folan was sure of it. Tyranny was just a difficult personality trait to convey while floating in midair.

Folan anchored herself to her science station by curling her fingers under the lip of one scanner console. "Gravity systems have lost battery power, sir. Engineering is trying to route power from secondary batteries, but the relays are off-line."

"If this is Picard's weapon, why is he not gloating?" J'emery spat the question, rather literally, and a small bubble of saliva became a globe of liquid that floated before his nose until he angrily batted it out of his line of sight. "This is maddening!"

"Yes, sir," Folan said. "It is possible the *Enterprise* is going through similar malfunctions. Their communications signal was not on a subspace frequency. Perhaps because they knew our subspace communications were down, or perhaps because they've lost that capability as well." Her hair had come undone from its arrangement and was floating wildly above and in front of her. Suddenly she wished she'd chosen a shorter style last time she was cutting her hair. "I don't believe the Federation would break the peace. It is not their—"

"Spare me your theories, Folan! If gravity control cannot be restored in a timely fashion, then issue the bridge magnetic boots. One or the other, *now!*"

"Yes, sir." Folan issued a command into a small communicator she wore on her uniform tunic. When she turned back, her commander had righted himself and was using his tight fists to moor himself to the command chair.

He didn't like her, and she knew it. To a degree, she even understood it. The mission on which his ship was about to embark was for *her* experiments and tests. She had supplanted his usual science officer, and his orders were to help her study. He would have rather been on patrol.

"How much life support have we left?" he barked.

Folan checked a flickering screen on her console. "Forty-three minutes, seventeen seconds."

His face flushed green with anger, probably at Picard, but also at Folan—not to mention the universe at large. J'emery seemed to be keeping himself from ranting. Instead he merely growled his next order. "Get a weapon on-line. Any weapon at all."

Chapter Two

Scientific Center Prime
Caltiska IV
Caltiskan Star System—bordering
  Romulan Empire–claimed space

"WHAT WAS THAT? Did you feel that?" Varnell was a centurion, and though he only looked young, he often seemed unsophisticated. He asked too many questions, and while his skills and qualifications had checked out, T'sart hadn't liked him from the moment they'd met.

"Yes, I felt that," Commander T'sart said calmly as he viewed one screen, then another, finding the alien console far less complex than his first glimpse two weeks ago. "There has been a change in subspace resonance frequencies. Such interesting technology. We don't even have sensors that scan at this level."

His upswept brows knitted in angst, Varnell had a film of perspiration above his lip. "These frequencies are far-reaching. We could be affecting subspace as far away as the homeworld. And we're not in space—we should not even be able to feel such a vibration on a planet."

They were indeed on a planet, if it could be called that. A ball of rock that shouldn't even exist by every law of physics T'sart knew, a few of which he'd written himself. They'd put him in this system thinking the planet uninhabited and worthless. It was neither.

He keyed another command into the console, and they both felt that vibration again, only stronger. He needed to pay more attention to what he was doing. It wouldn't be good to destroy this dry, foul little planet, at least not until he was no longer standing on it.

"Sir," Varnell said, "as I said, it is likely these vibrations are traveling outside this system and are not local. We are increasing the spatial distortions rather than decreasing them. We should not have pulled the sphere."

"I'm well aware of the situation, Varnell," T'sart sighed. "The disruptions may be far-reaching, but any disruption now will soon be controlled. *If* we finish these tests."

Had it not been for the centurion's credentials in so many areas of subspace mechanics, T'sart would not have tolerated the spineless man on his staff at all.

The sub-commander in charge of securing the city walked in, and T'sart automatically encrypted his console's controls before he turned away. It was a habit he'd learned early in his career, and never forgot.

"Report," he ordered, and hoped the news was good. Since they'd arrived more than two months ago, the native population had fought to the death to protect their science facility. Two weeks ago, when they lost it to T'sart and his forces, they'd fought even harder. It was as if they knew what they had, but their own technology was such that they surely could not. Perhaps in myth and legend they knew what it did for them, but probably nothing more.

"Commander, the perimeter is secure." The man still wore his battle helm. Here was someone T'sart could give some small measure of respect: strong, somewhat intelligent, and while no doubt still a fool in many ways, he at least had the courage to join his men in battle.

"Excellent."

"The alien death toll is estimated at forty-four thousand."

"Indeed?" T'sart asked, entering calculations into a tricorder. *"We're* the aliens here. This is *their* planet."

"Sir?" the sub-commander asked.

"The term you're looking for is 'native,' not alien."

Nodding slowly, the man didn't seem to truly absorb the lesson. "Yes, Commander."

"I don't want estimates. I want actual numbers." T'sart handed him the tricorder. "Use this. It will scan for a common strand of their DNA, and then verify if the owner of that strand is alive or dead."

The man took the instrument and reviewed the settings. "This . . . this is ingenious."

"Of course. Dismissed."

They exchanged nods, and the sub-commander exited the control room.

"A bit bloodthirsty, aren't you?" Varnell asked.

A mysterious moment for him to grow a backbone. "No one complained when it was my job to rid the empire of the four-hundred-and-four thousand, three-hundred-and-ninety-two inhabitants of Qu'takt III," T'sart said, sure to keep his tone even, though inside he seethed. "I heard no insults of bloodlust when it fell to me to design a genetic disease that could kill three different races in a matter of weeks, and then biodegrade into a minor illness for any Romulan who stumbled upon it. All I heard then were accolades and tributes."

"I meant no offense, Commander," Varnell murmured.

T'sart smiled warmly. "Of course not." He was bitter, yes . . . but acrimony was no tool of persuasion. If anything, his new situation demanded he be more persuasive than ever. "And I took no offense." But he did. He took offense at Varnell, and at all those in the Senate who'd been so close to giving him up. And who had eventually put him in this hind end of space, thinking T'sart would be forgotten. He refused.

Varnell nodded slowly in acceptance, but looked somewhat uncomfortable.

T'sart pondered attempting to soothe Varnell's ruffled feathers, but the door to the control room slid open and one of the Caltiskan survivors skittered in. He collapsed a meter from T'sart's feet.

"Does this belong to you?" In walked a tall, thin Romulan, his dark cloak impeccably crisp and clean. Obviously he'd been the one to throw the Caltiskan onto the floor.

With a flutter of his fingers, T'sart finished his encryption code and turned toward the man. "And you are . . ."

The intruder ignored T'sart's question and looked at Varnell. "Leave," he ordered.

Varnell nodded to the man and promptly left without giving T'sart, his commander, a second look. That bothered T'sart a bit. He found it rude and disloyal. But perhaps the centurion was frightened. The tall man was, after all, Tal Shiar.

"Your name was . . ." T'sart prodded again.

The Tal Shiar agent stared at him for a moment, then began to walk the room, looking intently at every item of equipment and every computer console. "Why did you leave this one alive?" he asked, motioning toward the Caltiskan.

T'sart said nothing for a moment, then finally spoke. "Even for Tal Shiar, you're rather humorless."

In a deep baritone, a product of his height, the man simply said, "Answer my question."

There was a time when T'sart had been asked to join the Tal Shiar. He'd refused. That was not completely unheard of in the Empire, but . . . almost. It had shocked the agent who'd approached him, and the Tal Shiar didn't like to be shocked. Later, he'd heard that the agent in question had been executed for not turning T'sart, but no one had ever approached him again. Had he joined them all those years ago, he would probably have outranked the agent before him now. *Well,* T'sart thought, smiling, *there are other ways to be someone's superior.*

"What is your authorization to ask questions of me?" T'sart asked. Too important to just kill, he knew the agent would have to at least *listen* to the questions, if not answer them.

Before the Tal Shiar agent had a chance to reply—as if he actually would have—the sub-commander entered again.

He was looking down at his tricorder. "Commander, I have the final death toll. Total native casualties: forty-three thousand, seven-hundred-thirty-two." The "two" trailed off as he looked up and saw only T'sart and the member of the Tal Shiar.

The agent looked at the sub-commander intently. The sub-commander nodded quickly, pivoted on a heel, and left.

The automatic door closed swiftly behind him.

The Tal Shiar agent curled around back to T'sart. "Why has this one been left alive?"

"He failed to tell me what I wanted to know," T'sart said finally, hating to be without acceptable choices. "But I thought he might yet be of use."

In a motion that could best be described as a glide, the agent moved toward the whimpering man, who was still cowering on the floor. "Tell him what he wants to know."

T'sart shook his head. "He will not talk for you. He doesn't *know* your reputation, and I've already made him aware of mine."

"I cannot help you," the Caltiskan said, muffling his sobs. "You will destroy our world."

"Your world should have been destroyed a billion

years ago," T'sart told him. "I'm beginning to think even *you* don't know why it wasn't."

"I implore you," the Caltiskan pleaded. "I *beg* of you."

The agent frowned and shook his head. "You'll not get him to talk," he decided.

"Perhaps not," T'sart admitted. "But I'm having several small children who survived the bioweapon gathered—"

In a swift arc of his right arm, the Tal Shiar agent pulled out his disrupter, fired, and returned the weapon to his cloak.

"A waste of time," he said as the Caltiskan shrieked into nothingness, his body vaporizing, his voice lingering as echo. "Your count is now forty-three thousand, seven-hundred-thirty-three."

"Yes." T'sart glowered. "And *now* I suppose it would be a waste of time." He sighed. "That man was the director of this facility. Sooner or later, he would have cracked, and been of use."

The Tal Shiar agent walked past him and began investigating the main computer and sensor consoles. "It is no longer your concern. You are relieved here."

Deep within himself, T'sart exploded. But he contained it, turned it in on itself, and though inwardly he churned, on the surface he was calm and seemingly imperturbable. "I'd ask by whose authority, but I'll assume that's a classified Tal Shiar secret."

Without nodding, the agent somehow managed to convey a nonverbal affirmation. He then added, "As of now, everything about this project is a state secret."

In a brief, weak moment, T'sart actually attempted debate. "This is my discovery. I am familiar—"

The Tal Shiar silenced him with a glare. "The last person I met who was familiar with this facility is now vapor and ozone. Leave the troops, take your assistants, and return to the homeworld. Your work here is ended."

Eyes narrowed, T'sart burned silently, but again refused any display of anger.

He marched to the main console, flipped a few switches, pulled a data crystal from his pocket and replaced it into the data bank.

"I expect you will not relay my official protest to your superior," he said as he turned toward the exit.

"Never speak of this place again," the agent called after him.

"Of course," T'sart replied. "Never."

"And, T'sart?"

He turned back toward the agent, a bit surprised at the use of his name without rank or title.

The Tal Shiar smirked. "Be grateful it is not forty-four thousand seven-hundred-thirty-four."

Personal Spacecraft *R'loga*
Uncharted space near the Caltiskan system
Bordering Romulan Empire–claimed space

"Lotre," T'sart called from the aft scanner console. "Transfer power from shields to sensors. We must break through this interference."

T'sart saw his other assistant stiffen at the suggestion. "Something on your mind, Varnell?" he asked.

Hesitating a moment, Varnell only spoke once Lotre was looking away. "We have been ordered out of the area by the Tal Shiar. To stay—"

"Think, Centurion. The local subspace interference will mask us from their detection." T'sart kept himself from snapping at Varnell, but only barely. The rage was difficult to contain, given the circumstances, even for someone with his mental discipline.

The Empire had betrayed him, disloyally sticking him in a thankless and uninteresting job where he suffered the buffoons in the defense ministry. He had led offensive weapons research for thirty-five years, and now . . . now he'd been cast away again. Just as he had discovered what could be the power to rule the galaxy.

And that was the scope of it; he'd confirmed it. That the Tal Shiar had suddenly involved themselves only demonstrated how right he was. They knew it would make them gods. But they were ill-suited to such a role. T'sart was not.

"The Tal Shiar will not bother us, I assure you."

Varnell nodded, seemingly unconvinced. "Yes, sir," he replied nonetheless.

"I cannot pierce the special disruptions around the sphere," Lotre said, turning from his sensor console. "I'm having trouble enough with the local disruptions. Feedback has burned out the main sensor relays. Again. And we've depleted our reserve stores."

"So we've burned them out." T'sart pivoted toward him. "Do you understand the power here? Do you understand the level of technological sophistication?"

"*I* do," Varnell said.

Ever unimpressed with ill-timed sycophantic blatherings, T'sart challenged him. "Really, Varnell? Tell us why you think so."

"I . . . I knew it when we saw their entire military was protecting the one science complex."

T'sart wagged a lecturing finger. "You knew then it was important to *them*. But not that it would be important to *us*."

Respectful, but with a guarded tone, Varnell proceeded on an unexpected tack. " 'Us' meaning the Empire, or meaning those of us on this vessel?"

"Are you challenging my loyalty, Centurion?" T'sart looked at him quizzically, as if the young centurion had grown a second head. "Just what are you asking? I've assessed my duty to the Praetor. Have you? We've lost much in helping the Federation with their war against the Dominion. We are weak. Do you think I would seek to bolster myself and not my comrades?"

For a very long moment Varnell was silent. Whether it was from internal debate on the issue, or simply whether to speak at all, T'sart was unsure. "That is," he finally said, slowly, "with all due respect, sir, not what I meant." And then he lowered his head and his voice. "You are as loyal to the Empire as I, I'm sure of it."

"You're uncomfortable, Varnell. Why?" T'sart stepped closer to him.

The centurion glanced at Lotre. "Why do we discuss such matters in *his* presence?"

Why, indeed, T'sart thought, *are we discussing this at all?* "Lotre is a Romulan. As loyal as I am."

"He is a Klingon," Varnell said emphatically.

"Genetically, yes. But that is all."

"That is *all* they are," the young Romulan spat. "Genetic dispositions to rage and murder."

T'sart was droll. "How scientific of you."

As if suddenly remembering something, Varnell's attitude shifted into reverse. "I am sorry for speaking out of turn."

"Not at all," T'sart said nonchalantly. "But know that I trust Lotre's loyalty. And surely you trust mine as much as I trust yours, correct?" He leaned down a bit, looking into Varnell's eyes and studying his slightest expression.

"Of course, Commander." The centurion would probably not have looked nervous to most. But T'sart knew people. He'd seen people at their best, and at their worst. Especially their worst. He could read a man almost as well as an empath.

After a moment, T'sart nodded to himself. He leaned over Varnell's shoulder and tapped into one of the control consoles.

Varnell turned quickly, reaching to push T'sart away, but it was too late. His face contorted in shock and anger as he flashed into a sparkle, and then dematerialized.

There was silence as Lotre left his station and joined T'sart near the main view port.

"You should have let me stab him," Lotre said.

T'sart shrugged. "This was less messy."

Lotre huffed. "And less fun."

The corners of T'sart's lips curled upward as first Varnell's leg floated past the port window, then his left arm, then part of his torso, then finally his horrific, frozen visage.

"Oh, I don't know about that."

Lotre chuckled darkly. "You doubted his loyalty this much?"

Alone with only Lotre, T'sart felt free to show his true rage. "He knew!" he yelled, turning back toward the helm. "I watched his eyes, and he knew!"

"Who knew?" Lotre asked.

"The Tal Shiar agent," T'sart hissed. "He entered and knew where every console was, what every control panel did! And only this dim-witted centurion, only Varnell could have provided the Tal Shiar with that information!"

"I've never seen you this way." Lotre didn't back away, but did seat himself in the nearest chair.

T'sart barely noticed. "I've never been this close!" He pounded a fist on the bulkhead and the vibration rumbled through the deckplates. "Disloyalty! I loathe it! I gave years to the Empire, and they nearly hand me over to a Federation/Klingon tribunal! And now *this?*"

"But they did not—"

Lips curling in burning indignation, T'sart slammed himself into the helm seat and bludgeoned the console before him. "No, they reduced my power instead. Putting me in a useless defense position, ignoring my past work, and squandering my talents. It took half my influence, half the favors owed me, to get this pitiful result. You *know* that!" He turned back toward Lotre.

"And you know I struggled back. With this, *this* discovery . . . it is mine. The Empire cannot have it."

"The Tal Shiar are a shadow empire unto themselves. I doubt the Senate is even aware—"

Cocking his head to one side, T'sart suddenly had one of those brilliant flashes he'd come to love about himself, the rush of adrenaline when it dawned on him what he must do—and *could* do. "You're right, my friend," he said, regaining his composure. "You're right. The Tal Shiar would not have informed the Senate. They know, and we know, and no one else does."

A bit taken aback, a strange emotion to see on such a Klingon face, Lotre narrowed his brow. "You intend to make war against the Tal Shiar?"

T'sart nodded slowly. "Yes, I believe I do."

Lotre scoffed. "Tal Shiar agents are everywhere. You won't be able to just requisition one warbird, never mind the two or more we would need."

With a smirk that could have cut neutronium, the Romulan ground out a mirthful whisper. "We won't need a warbird. Not when we can have a very strong and very powerful starship. And I know just where to find one."

Chapter Three

Romulan Neutral Zone
Section 19

"SIR, I CANNOT EXPLAIN THIS. It makes no logical sense." From Data, that was quite a thing to hear.

Picard glanced up at the silent warp engine core. Normally it would be thrumming with energy, with raw, focused power. It should be that way now, but wasn't. Why?

Geordi La Forge slithered out of a Jefferies tube to Data's right and walked over to the console next to the android. He tapped harshly at the controls. "Still nothing, sir. Zero." In the three years since Geordi had exchanged his VISOR for the more natural-looking optical implants that also allowed him to see, Picard

25

had become used to the man's wealth of expression, once so hidden. Now, his engineer's grayish eyes cast themselves down in frustration.

"Not sabotage," Picard said. Not if the Romulans were in the same boat. Seeing the warbird lose gravity . . . well, there was something more wrong than could be simply explained away with an answer of sabotage. Something large, Picard thought, and felt a rock of tension rolling around his gut.

"If it was sabotage, I don't know how," La Forge said. "This *should* be working. There's no reason we shouldn't have power—we just don't. I mean, this isn't just not being able to create a warp field. We can't generate enough power to heat a cup of coffee. Not unless we drain a battery."

"It would seem," Data said with deliberate slowness, "some sort of . . . field, perhaps . . . is inhibiting high-energy power consumption and," he raised his brows, "even creation. I believe it is localized to this area of space. How far it extends, we do not know."

"How are *you* now, Data?" Picard asked, allowing himself the slightest edge of concern in his voice.

The android seemed to consider the question a long moment. His yellow color probably was no paler than usual, but Picard thought he appeared somewhat more sallow than was the norm. "I suppose the best way to describe it, sir, is 'under the weather.' My power source is similar to that of many of the ship's systems. Just as the *Enterprise* computers are running on battery backup, so am I, essentially."

A strange thing to have a member of one's crew tell you. "How long can you . . . maintain that?"

"At full capacity? A limited amount of time without internal recharge, sir. At this level of operation, for me, perhaps a few years."

"You said perhaps a dampening field . . ."

"Possibly, sir," Data said. He looked tired. "Conjecture, since we cannot detect such a field. Sensors are semi-operative, but I find nothing unusual as of yet. We have confirmed that the Romulan ship is in a similar situation, and the cargo vessel is completely dead in space."

"Let's hope some life support on the cargo ship is working. What about the warbird? What systems have they up and running?"

Data shook his head. "Scans are not precise at these low power levels."

Picard turned in thought, glancing at an engineering station that was dark, of necessity, to conserve power. "In any case, it's not the Romulans' doing. And whatever is happening isn't limited to this vessel. Assuming the Romulans aren't deceiving us by pretending to have similar power troubles . . ."

La Forge nodded. "Lucky for us if they're not."

The captain pressed out a breath into a sigh. "Being stranded in the Neutral Zone doesn't feel particularly lucky, Mr. La Forge. Even with the recent tone of accord." He tapped a command into the console before them, then had to type in an access password to bypass the power restrictions in effect. "If this problem is localized to this region of space . . . We began losing power here," Picard said, pointing at an area of the graphic he'd requested from the computer. "Let's assume whatever is causing this doesn't have an effect outside a certain perimeter. Let's also assume that if we go back the way we came our ability to generate power will return as well."

"Those are a lot of assumptions, sir," Data said.

"I'm open to a better suggestion, Mr. Data."

The android looked to La Forge, then back to the captain. "I have none, sir. But maneuvering with only chemical thrusters—"

"Yes," Picard said gravely, turning off the monitor before him. "Retracing an impulse-speed journey with only thrusters would take days."

"Sixty-two point three two days, sir," Data said.

Only two decimal places. Data *was* weak.

The captain looked up again at the looming, silent engine core. Picard was used to having the power of a hundred suns at his fingertips. The laws of physics said he still did. At least the laws he *knew* said that. There was a mystery here, and he wanted to solve it for more reasons then just freeing his ship from the flypaper they'd been glued to. "Well, gentlemen," he said matter-of-factly, "I suggest we find a nonengine alternative to propulsion."

"Nonengine propulsion, sir?" La Forge asked. "There isn't a solar sail big enough to move the *Enterprise* at the speed we'll need to—"

"No, Commander. I have another idea. If the Romulans will help."

La Forge's eyes grew wide, then became a disbelieving squint. "I don't like this plan already."

* * *

"Of course, Captain." J'emery chuckled humorlessly. "I'm certain the only solution to our situation is for me to allow your engineers access to my ship's most critical systems. Will your doctor need to perform an operation on *me* as well? What about my crew?" Suddenly the Romulan commander's false smile was gone. "Should I have every third man commit suicide so as to save room in your brig?"

Picard sighed inwardly and glanced back to Deanna Troi, ship's counselor, empath, and confidant.

"He's taking this better than you thought," she offered, then looked to Riker for agreement.

"Much."

The captain grunted a nod and turned back to the forward viewscreen and J'emery's angry visage.

"You know as well as I do that this isn't a trap set by either of us. Our respective governments have been working together for months. The trade embargo between our governments has been lifted. We have no quarrel with you. And if our goal *was* to destroy your vessel, and we'd laid this snare, you would've been killed by now. I'll assume the reverse is true as well. Our subspace communications are down, so we'll also assume neither of us is waiting on fleet support. However, we've launched a communications buoy and confirmed to Starfleet our position and situation. Doing that also verified that approximately four light minutes from our respective positions this . . . dampening field, whatever it is, weakens enough for normal power systems to come on-line. We can sit here and argue, or we can both help one another end this situation peacefully." The captain walked slowly back to his command chair, lowering himself down with just the slightest adjustments to his uniform tunic. "I realize our personal trust factor isn't especially high, no matter what our governments may have agreed to. I'm willing to shuttle aboard your ship myself, bring the parts necessary, and help with the required modifications." He nodded. "More reassurance than that, I cannot offer."

Gravity restored, Sub-Commander Folan was able to easily step to her commander's side. "You accepted the *Enterprise*'s proposition more rapidly than I expected."

J'emery smiled. "Yes, I did. But Picard is too gullible to see that. We have enough power for disruptors?"

Folan nodded, her superior's treachery now clear. "Yes, Commander. Two short bursts."

"Excellent. One for Picard's shuttle, another for *Enterprise* herself. And they are without shields. . . ." His eyes a bit gleeful, J'emery pounded his fist lightly on the arm of his command chair. "With Picard gone, and the *Enterprise* further disabled, the Praetor will have a nice prize when we return home."

"If I may, Commander," Folan said. "This is directly against current Senate policy with regard to Federation vessels. As well, I believe the *Enterprise* is truly offering a means of escape for us both. I've gone over their data—"

"Science is your strength, Folan, but tactics are not. You are as gullible as Picard."

Folan pursed her lips and stifled a retort that would

not serve her well. She had long tired of hearing she was just a science officer and not a Romulan military officer in full. There were other ways to serve the Empire and the Romulan people, she thought. That such ways were deemed unimportant was foolhardy and . . . well, it annoyed her. "How else might we restore our powerless systems?"

"Even without communications from us, we will be missed. In a day, at the most, a ship will be searching for us," J'emery said, dismissing her concern with a wave of his hand.

"I fear life support will not last that long, Commander. Especially if we divert battery power to the weapons array."

J'emery turned directly toward her as he rose from his seat. "You have your orders, Folan. When Picard is halfway here, destroy his shuttle. Then target the *Enterprise* and disable their remaining systems."

A shuttle, dragging with thrusters only—without shields, without weapons, without much of anything but life support and a crawling speed. There were tests like this at the Academy, Picard thought, boring little exercises about running in minimal power under adverse circumstances. This was why. What they didn't train him for was the frustration of being a starship captain who was used to riding a stallion, and now had to suffer on the back of a mule.

All this for one cargo vessel that had strayed off course . . . perhaps. There was no firm data on the cargo hauler. It was out of sensor range, out of visual range . . . Picard only hoped the ship was undamaged and recoverable.

He thumbed a panel. "Picard to *Enterprise*."

"Shapiro here, sir."

"Patch me into the Romulan vessel, Ensign."

"Aye, sir."

J'emery's stern features appeared on Picard's small viewscreen. "Captain?" The Romulan's tone had a bitter edge, and his expression was that of someone who'd tasted wine gone to vinegar.

"Since we'll need all available power for your tractor beams, I'd rather dock manually. Is that acceptable to you?"

The Romulan smiled an odd little smile. "That will be acceptable, Captain Picard. Very."

The screen went blank.

"Lock disruptors on target," J'emery ordered.

The weapons officer shook his head. "Target lock unavailable, Commander. Sensors hampered, unknown cause."

J'emery frowned. "Manual target," he spat. "And don't miss."

Folan had never been fond of J'emery, but he was being especially mush-headed today, she thought. She didn't trust Picard fully, but she knew the science of what he proposed, and the science was sound.

Of course, there was no scientific explanation for all that had happened to their respective ships. At least not yet.

She ran the power-consumption projections again.

There might be enough power for life support, but all that depended on when another ship would arrive. As it was, they had another forty-three minutes of life support. If they crowded the crew into a common area and shut down all other systems, maybe that would give them two days. Maybe. And that was only if they didn't use any of their weapons. Command or not, J'emery's was a fool's decision.

Really, Picard's plan was the only foreseeable way. Each ship would be able to tractor the other, using one another as a mass with which to propel the opposite ship out of the . . . "power desert," for lack of a better term. The *Enterprise* would pull the *Makluan* past itself, flinging the Romulan warbird out of the desert, and the *Makluan* would do the same for *Enterprise,* propelling the Federation ship out in the opposite direction. Without the power of the other ship, no one ship would be able to escape alone.

Her commander was blind to it, though. And so what could she do but sit and watch? In moments Picard would be dead and their chance would be lost. He brought with him the power coupling that would allow battery power to be transferred to the tractor beams. All battery power . . . meaning that if this didn't work, there'd be nothing left for life support, let alone weapons.

Yes, it was all a risk. But . . . the science worked. The plan would work. It *had* to.

Folan's eyes lingered on the weapon's control console. She could bleed away the power from here, make it become lost in the system. With all that's happened, it would be a mystery. No one would be blamed.

Her fingers brushed the panel.

It would be so easy.

She glanced at J'emery, and then at the weapons officer across the bridge.

Mutiny. Treason. She could be put to death for this, slowly.

Or . . . she could not do it, and likely asphyxiate with her crew. Loyal, but dead.

Those were her choices now: ardent but extinct, or disloyal and perhaps . . . well, perhaps still dead.

She chose.

"Fire," J'emery ordered.

"Yes, Commander. We—Sir, I don't have power." The weapons officer was incredulous, of course. Not only had Folan put her own life at risk, but his as well. If J'emery blamed the weapons officer . . .

Commander J'emery said nothing. Yet, if focused, his glare alone could have destroyed Picard's shuttle.

"Welcome the captain aboard when he docks, and see that he's treated with respect," the commander growled to Folan. "I want him guarded at all times," he added, then turned to the weapons officer. "You're reduced a step in rank and confined to your quarters. Dismissed."

He turned to Folan. "Sub-Commander!"

Nervously, she stepped forward. Did he know?

"Why?" he demanded. "I want to know *why*. And you're going to find out. How did this happen to the power? And when we know who to blame, I will deal with them personally."

"Yes, Commander."

"Find out, quickly," he barked.

Folan nodded, then breathed a sigh of relief as she left the bridge. She'd gotten away with a crime most high, and had perhaps slipped her neck out of a very confining noose. For now, she thought, and suppressed a shudder. Only for now.

It hadn't taken as long as Picard expected. Romulan technology was different, but not too different in the area of tractor beams and power conduits. Within thirty minutes he was on the Romulan bridge, meeting J'emery face to face. Folan, the science officer and the person who'd supervised Picard's work and aided him at times as well, had been distant, if civil. She'd complimented his plan, although he was sure to explain that, while it was his idea, the details of implementation belonged to his chief engineer. She'd nodded rather coldly at the time, but seemed to appreciate his humility. But now, on the bridge, she seemed even more detached.

"We're ready when you are," Riker said, his image shaky and static-peppered on the Romulan main view screen.

Picard looked to Folan, who nodded. J'emery seemed curious, anxious. He expected a trick of some kind, no doubt.

"We are ready, Commander," Folan told J'emery.

"Fine. Initiate at will."

There was a brief countdown and then a crackling noise as the Romulan vessel shook around them.

"We *are* moving," Folan said, apparently a bit surprised. "*Enterprise* is drawing us toward them, and they toward us."

Slowly at first, but gaining speed as they went, the warbird and *Enterprise* moved toward each other, pulling one another closer and closer until they veered apart, pushing off and away.

But the tractor beams drained the last bit of power. The Romulan viewscreen went dark first. Then the control consoles. Then the lights.

The din of Romulan crew voices was too fast for the universal translator to handle. Picard turned in the dark on an unfamiliar bridge and thought he bumped into a guardrail, or perhaps a guard.

Then the lights returned, as did the hum of the control circuits and panels.

The captain had bumped into Folan, who was hunched over her now-active console.

"It has worked," she said, more animated than Picard had heard her until then. "We are clear of the dead zone and power is returning to normal output levels. Batteries are recharging. *Enterprise* is clear as well. Sensors are on-line."

Picard's lips curled up just a touch. "Thank you for your help. We couldn't have done this without your keen knowledge."

"You have no idea," Folan said, straightening, her eyes striking out toward him, lingering a moment, then looking quickly down.

Picard furrowed his brows. There was something in her tone, in that look . . . something that sold the idea that Picard was in *her* debt, and not the other way around.

"Thank you, Captain," J'emery said. "But we still have the matter of this treaty violation, since the new treaties have not been registered yet in our official records—"

He motioned for his guards.

"I'm sure," Picard said, "that will be handled in the upper echelons of the diplomatic services, Commander." He tapped his comm badge. "Picard to *Enterprise.* Beam me out."

A familiar hum filled the air.

"Wait, Captain—" J'emery demanded.

Too late. Picard dematerialized in a wash of sparkle and light.

"He plotted that! Deceitful, manipulative Terrans!"

Folan bent over her console again. "They've also beamed out their shuttle." Inwardly, she smiled. Picard did trust, but neither was he a fool. Had the situation been reversed, she might have done the same.

J'emery was furious. There was little to substantiate holding Picard or *Enterprise,* but he'd have done it anyway, just to see if he could learn anything new about the Federation ship or her crew.

Folan could see in her commander's eyes that he wanted to fire on *Enterprise.* She considered counseling him against it. Or for it. Whatever might put her in his good graces. Of course, she was but his science officer and not a military advisor, so no recommendation would go without punishment.

She stayed silent, as did J'emery, fuming.

* * *

Picard materialized on his own bridge. "Status report, Number One."

"Power is back on all levels, sir, as if someone flipped a switch. Batteries are recharging."

"Excellent."

"We aim to please." Riker smiled and vacated the command chair.

"Can we get a sensor lock on the cargo ship?" The captain lowered himself into his command chair. "We need to find a way to haul—"

"Captain," Chamberlain said, "I can barely read the cargo vessel, sir, but . . ." He paused.

"Lieutenant? " Eyes darting up, Picard watched the viewer as the drifting form of the cargo hauler appeared on the screen.

"No life-signs, sir. No power."

"Heat output—"

"Negative, sir."

Picard shared a glance with Riker, then with Troi.

No heat. No life. Probably hadn't been for some time.

The captain rose. "All dead. In the dead zone," Picard murmured.

Now Riker stood. "The what?"

Dead zone. It was what Folan had called it. And it fit. Phasers, disruptors . . . none of their most powerful technology worked there. Not even life support, once batteries had drained. A hole in physics you couldn't drive a starship through.

"How many people . . ." Picard began to ask, but the actual number was almost meaningless. One was enough. He almost didn't want to know how many more than one had been lost.

What he did want to know, more than anything, was *why*.

And the answer sat in the middle of unreachable, dead space.

Chapter Four

**Federation Starship *Exeter*
Alpha Quadrant
Unexplored sector**

Nineteen days ago

"WHERE'S THAT AUXILIARY POWER?" Captain James Venes anxiously scratched the back of his neck as he made his way down toward the command chair.

"Aux power's not responding. Batteries only, sir."

"Is Ortiz in Engineering yet? What's going on down there?" The captain thumbed a button on the command chair, but did not lower himself into the seat. "Venes to Engineering. We've lost helm control now, people."

"Ortiz here, sir. I can't explain it. There's no reason—"

"I don't need a reason, Alvaro, I just need power before we lose life support. Batteries won't last long with all these refugees on board."

Venes heard his engineer breathe out a slight sigh. *"Aye, sir."*

"Hey, if anyone can lick this problem, it's you. Let me know when you have something. Venes out." The small pep talk seemed uninspirational, even desperate. The captain knew it, but there just wasn't much to say. His people knew their jobs, and they'd do them for duty, not kudos.

Finally setting himself into the command chair, Venes tried to relax his body, if not his mind. He couldn't. He was getting too old for this, he chided himself. Too old for deep space and mystery. Too old for refugees and missions away from Jenny. Too old to die because someone forgot to pay his starship's electric bill.

"Send out a log buoy," he ordered finally. "And let's make sure our passengers don't panic, but see if we can cram them into some more confined accommodations. Crew, too. Conserve as much energy as possible." He hit the intercom again. At least that was still working. For now. "Engineering."

"Ortiz here, sir."

"Alvaro, what about other sources of battery power on the ship?"

"Other sources, sir?"

"Yeah. Batteries from shuttles, runabouts, whatever."

There was a brief pause as Ortiz considered it. *"Yes, sir. Will take some doing, but we can rig that up. Won't buy us a lot of time, but some."*

"Take the batteries from the escape pods, too, Alvaro."

A much longer pause. Venes thought his engineer might be considering confirming the order.

"We don't even have enough pods, with all the refugees on board. Might as well do all we can to save the ship."

"*Aye, sir.*"

"Venes out."

"Sir?" said the ops officer. "Decks seven and eight have lost all power."

Venes almost sighed, but decided against it. "Understood," he said finally. It was one thing to lose power when under attack, but such a sudden loss of functionality . . . Sure, he told his engineer he didn't care what had caused it, but of course he *did* care, since that would tell them how to fix it and keep it from happening again. He hoped.

In the back of his mind he remembered something similar happening just a day or two ago. He hadn't read the full report, just skimmed it because he was tired. If the computers were working, he'd simply call it up, but no such luck today. Rubbing his temple thoughtfully, Venes searched his memory a long moment, then recalled a detail or two.

"*Enterprise,*" he murmured, but remembering did him little good. He did seem to recall something about needing two ships to solve the problem, and so he was short one vessel for such work.

The lights dimmed, and the captain thought perhaps he was short more than one ship. Perhaps he needed help from two.

They'd try to come up with some other alternative. They'd do everything possible to find some answer . . . but something told Venes that there was little to do now but wait . . . either for help to arrive, or for death.

Personal Spacecraft *R'loga*
Jacaria system—Romulan space
Orbiting Moon of Jacaria VII

"Are you sure?" T'sart asked again. Rarely did he show such an imperfection as shock. But he *was* shocked, and if Lotre saw it . . . well, he would be the only one T'sart would trust to witness his faults.

"I am sure," Lotre said. "Varnell was a member of the Tal Shiar . . . and we killed him." The Klingon smoothed the traditional Romulan tunic that stretched over his broad shoulders.

We. Even in these harsh times, Lotre was loyal. The Praetor and the Senate were not. T'sart seethed with hatred, for them and for the dead Tal Shiar spy.

"Poor timing," T'sart said finally as he paced the meager length of the small ship. Four bulkheads, one room, two days on this blasted ship. He was used to a bedroom this large. He hated being confined, and it was beginning to grate on his nerves.

"Had he had time to fully encrypt his last message to them, we might never have known. I'd say your timing was impeccable, as always." Lotre tucked a padd into a case and put it on the deck as T'sart paced past it. "Knowing that the Tal Shiar will be after you for killing their operative, are you sure you want to follow through with this plan?"

Stopping, a brief smile passing his lips, T'sart asked, "Are you afraid of the Tal Shiar?"

Lotre was grim. "I'm afraid that *you* are not."

"We continue with my plans," T'sart said, "with just a few deviations."

The Klingon of Romulan upbringing waited, and when T'sart said no more, he prodded him. "And those are?"

"Well, the best way for the Tal Shiar to not waste resources on me . . . is for them to think me dead."

"But you won't be dead."

"Perish the thought," T'sart said with a smile.

Romulan Homeworld
City of Chaladra
Two blocks off Talar Street

Seventeen days ago

If there was anything T'sart liked less than a blindly loyal Romulan, it was a foolishly disloyal one. That's why he didn't mind if the boy died slowly. He preferred it, even, getting a certain satisfaction from the suffering. Especially considering all the trouble T'sart had had to put up with: an area of the city he would not usually go, the moist heat he hated so much in this province, and the type of people he had to deal with in order to remain generally unseen.

"And now, my youthful friend, die," T'sart whispered

as the boy, perhaps all of thirty-five years, withered out of his grip and slid down the stone wall.

"But . . . I told you and . . . you said you—"

T'sart smiled the smile that, after many years of practice, he knew to be both treacherous and gleeful. "Yes, yes, I did. And I lied. I tend to do that, m'boy."

He turned his grin to the small hypospray in his left hand. Another of his ingenious potions. This was better than the one he'd given to the government. He was careful to always keep a slightly more potent concoction for himself. He did that with anything he created for the Empire. His intellect was his own, and he would always see that the benefits of that were his before others'. Considering how he'd been treated recently, that was doubly wise.

As his prey finally perished, with a small puff of air from its lungs and the last of life's tension leaving its muscles, T'sart decided to leave the area quickly. There was a time he might have stayed to see to it that someone else was blamed for his doing. Not tonight. Tonight he had someone else to see . . . and the quest to conclude.

There he was, just down the hall, in the very simplest of offices. T'sart was careful not to allow his gaze to linger too long, but even if he had, the door opened and closed so quickly he probably would not have been seen.

After a short moment, he determinedly walked in the opposite direction, so as to not raise suspicion. Three days it had taken him to find this man, three days, and a cunning hunt. He had reason to be proud, as even the Tal Shiar had failed at this task, over and over and over again. *Tal Shiar,* he thought. *Simpletons, more con-*

cerned with their inner politics than anything of substance and import. I'll not see them take all my power.

Before reaching the entryway that would lead him back to the street, T'sart turned confidently and headed back toward the library, where he'd seen his long-sought prey. Why not confront now? All was in place, and he need not wait for the man to be alone. He *was* only a man. And T'sart could always *make* him alone, in any case.

Yes, in fact, that would be a very good idea. Let his ultimate prey know the ground rules.

The door was pushed out of T'sart's way with a firm hand and a slight creak. Perhaps the young guard recognized T'sart. Or perhaps duty alone called for him to raise a weapon to anyone who entered. In either case, he was too slow.

The second young Romulan to die this day was relieved of his weapon quickly, with a small but powerful twist to his wrist. The man across the room, the final prey, looked up from some text he was reading. T'sart could not help but smile. It *was* him.

T'sart looked back toward the guard, who did not yelp in pain, though he should have. There was no expression on the young man's face at all. No surprise, no terror. What trick was this? Why didn't he struggle or cry out?

It stunned T'sart, for just a moment, and he stared too long at the boy in his grip. When he looked up, the final prey was gone.

"No! Fool!" T'sart fired the weapon he'd taken two seconds before, firing point-blank at the boy's head.

The weapon was set to stun, of course, T'sart realized a moment later. Fine. A stun at such proximity and to the head would bring a slow, lingering death. He let the guard fall straight down as he quickly turned toward where the other had been.

"Where are you?" T'sart huffed under his breath. There was no place to hide in here, and no one could have gotten past T'sart to the door through which he'd just entered. There was another door on the other side of the room, but it had neither opened nor closed, and from where he stood he saw it was locked.

A hidden door? A transporter? Technically it could be either, but transporter beams were not widely used for intraplanetary purposes on the homeworld, and the energy surge would be noticed and draw suspicion.

The other door, T'sart decided, was his only choice.

Through it was another hallway with many tributaries. T'sart gnashed his teeth as he made his way slowly down the hallway, listening. Had he thought to bring a tricorder he would know where the man was now. But tricorders on average townspeople was questionable in itself, and he'd thought better of taking that risk.

There were no footsteps to be heard, and no breath save his own. Where could his prey have gone? *Where?*

Frustration trickled sweat down T'sart's neck. He damned himself for looking too long at the guard's expressionless face. Why had the guard not called out in pain or anger? Was he being taught, or was it a planned contrivance to confuse for just that moment?

Up one corridor and down the next, T'sart saw no sign of his final prey. None. And no doors that he could further check. If he had come this far only to lose the man . . . No. T'sart would not accept that. *He's here. Somewhere. Find him, before he finds you—*

"Cease. Turn slowly."

Too late.

"Very well." T'sart felt the disruptor that was now lightly pressed against his back, heard its soft, powerful hum. After a moment the pressure was gone. His prey had found him, announced his presence and advantage, then stepped out of striking distance. Smart, T'sart thought as he nodded, smiled thinly, and slowly turned toward his captor.

The man with the disruptor took T'sart's weapon and glanced over him, probably wondering what other devices should be found and confiscated.

T'sart smiled. "It would seem you have the advantage, Mister . . . do you have a name you'd prefer me to use?"

His captor raised one brow. "Subterfuge at this point seems futile. You know who I am."

T'sart nodded. "Yes, Spock. Yes, I do. Or shall I call you Ambassador? Or do you yearn for the days when you were Captain Spock?"

The Vulcan did not move, did not show surprise, did not show anything on that damned expressionless face.

"Why are you here?" Spock asked.

"To speak with you, of course."

Again, no expression. No irritation. Just Spock's bland tone. "My question required a more specific answer."

T'sart smiled. He hated Vulcans, but loved toying with them, and he'd been given only a few occasions over the years to do just that. So, fine, Spock showed no frustration. T'sart was surely being frustrating nevertheless. "Of course," he said finally, masking his tension with a false smile.

"Move down the corridor. Take the first turn on the left and then the door at the end of that hall," Spock ordered, but did not motion with his weapon hand.

With deliberate, perhaps almost Vulcan grace, T'sart did as he was ordered. Once in the room, he noticed the man he'd stunned just a few minutes before was gone. Spock had seen to him already, gotten him help, and still had time to turn the tables on T'sart.

Vulcans, T'sart thought bitterly.

"Sit."

Fine. The Romulan sat in a chair in front of what was presumably Spock's desk.

"State your purpose in contacting me."

T'sart paused, then finally began in what he hoped was an almost pleasant tone. "My business is urgent, but not so much that we must forget civilities. Allow me to savor the meeting, Spock. You have no idea how many people I've had to kill to gain your trail."

"Twelve, if young Polnor lives. State your purpose."

Suddenly T'sart's smile faded. He'd hoped the death toll would be thirteen soon, and had he not needed Spock so badly he would've liked the Vulcan to be the fourteenth victim.

"You're very intelligent," T'sart admitted. "Almost as intelligent as your reputation."

Spock kept his weapon aimed evenly. "I'm sure the reverse is true. Your purpose, T'sart."

It was the first time Spock had used T'sart's name, and for some reason it startled the Romulan a bit.

T'sart couldn't help then but notice that the Vulcan's Romulan accent was near perfect. He would've passed easily as a native. Obviously had.

"I want to defect to the Federation," T'sart said finally. "And I want you to help me."

Silently, Spock seemed to consider the veracity of T'sart's confession.

"You don't need to believe me, Spock. Either way, your task would be finished on this planet, if I chose it. You don't know how many people besides myself know of your presence here. Not just here on the home-world, but specifically here in this town, on this street, in this building, in this room, standing in that spot."

Spock nodded. "Perhaps."

Damned smug Vulcans. "Perhaps" killing you would be exquisite. "Perhaps indeed. Put down your weapon," T'sart ordered. "We have much to discuss."

Chapter Five

**Federation Research Colony on
  Gamma Hydra IV
Gamma Hydra Sector
Section 2**

Sixteen days ago

"I'M TELLING YOU, it's probably just another comet. You get them here all the time, right?"

Young Miko Tariki idolized Dr. Spurn, so the good doctor decided not to crush the new transfer with a few well-chosen words. Yes, the fresh-from-university man was imbecilic, but he agreed with every scientific paper written by J.B. Spurn, and so the boy had some promise, if little else.

"Planetary defense systems have taken care of two

comets in the last three years. Sensor stations throughout the system say we're clear," said K'leeta Mertal, head of research for the southern projects. Another imbecile heard from. She wouldn't know a comet if she was standing on its tail.

"One sensor buoy isn't responding," Spurn said. "Or did you forget that, my young flower?"

"Buoys fail all the time. There *is* sensor overlap." A beautiful woman, but Spurn had never seen her smile, not once, in his presence. "Or," she added, "did *you* forget that, my old weed?"

Petulant.

Horace Blake, colony leader—more a figurehead than a true decision-maker—finally stepped into the discussion he'd let meander for more than twenty minutes. "A starship will be by in three days for supplies and crew replacement. The—" Blake looked down at some notes, but didn't see the ship's name quickly enough.

"The *Dezago*," Spurn offered.

"Yes, the *Dezago*." Blake nodded.

Mertal pressed her lips into what Spurn figured was her version of a smile. "Why don't you go with the *Dezago*, J.B.? Get away for a month. Or two. Or twelve."

"As close as we are to the Romulan Neutral Zone, I *should* want to leave here. Who's to say our dead buoy isn't their doing?"

"We *are* very close to the Neutral Zone—" Tariki said.

"But Starbase 10—"

"Ignores us repeatedly, boy," Spurn scoffed.

"Well, they don't have their own starship, not since the *Stocker* was destroyed," one of the other, lesser members mumbled.

Spurn didn't know the person well, and didn't care to, he was sure. "We have a more immediate problem, ladies and gentlemen. We're running on batteries only."

"We have food stores to last us months," Blake said, glancing again at his notes. Chances are he didn't see that fact in his notes, and only used them to avoid the looks of others when he spoke. Spurn had yet to see the man look anyone straight in the eyes.

"I have several experiments that will falter when we lose the battery power to the labs," Spurn said. "There's a reason why there aren't *any* of the generators working, and we should find out what it is."

Mertel smiled. "You're a scientist, J.B., so you tell us."

"If I ever want to write a paper on arrogance, I know where I'll find my subject," Spurn said.

"A mirror? Or will you look in the holosuites?"

"Listen here, I've had it with—"

"Enough!" All were taken aback. Blake rarely yelled, and never became unpleasant. "I'm afraid this is the situation, people. Subspace communications *are* out and the *Dezago* isn't due for three more days. In that time, we may lose our research, but we won't lose our lives. I'd call that damned lucky."

"I'd call it—"

"No one cares what you'd call it, Spurn."

"Professor Blake, do I need to take this abuse?"

Some men are crushed by pressure. Others, pressure hardens and focuses them.

"Not at all," Blake said. "You're not required to be at these meetings at all."

Starfleet Sensor Monitoring Station
Sector 001-Sol III (Earth)
Detroit, Michigan

Sixteen days ago

"Oh, come on, Hedrick, you're not working on all thrusters with that one." Crewman Chris Spiker half chuckled, half winced at yet another of his chief's "supposin's."

"Hey, you don't need to believe me." Hedrick clicked buttons on his console with the ease of rote. "I'm just tellin' you what the reports say."

Spiker turned and picked up a padd. "Hmmmm . . ." He poured over the text with mock intensity. "The reports say four ships have lost power under mysterious circumstances. They say nothing about some hokey Romulan invasion plot."

Nodding matter-of-factly, Hedrick said, "You gotta learn to read *between* the lines, young'un. You been a sensor jockey for what? Five seconds? I been—"

"I spent thirteen months on the *Jenkins*."

"Science vessel," Hedrick scoffed. "And thirteen months ain't nothing. You're so damn young, I 'spect when you smile I don't know if somethin's funny or you got gas."

"Spare me the southern jibes, Chief. If you're so damn smart—" Spiker tossed the padd down and swiveled his chair toward the other console he needed to calibrate.

"Yup. Am smart. You don't think so? You tell me why four different ships in three days have had this power-loss thing. And all near the damn Romulan Neutral Zone."

"Yeah, yeah. There's no evidence—" Spiker turned back around.

Hedrick rolled his eyes. "Geez. There's no evidence of a cloaked ship until it's on top of you, is there? And I've heard about a few other things happening to other ships, a few Romulan colonies."

"You can't believe barroom talk from gossiping traders."

"*You* can't. I can. Nine times outta ten, it has a kernel of truth—"

This time Spiker was the one to roll his eyes. "See, listen to you: 'kernel of truth.' "

"You just gotta know what sounds plausible and what doesn't. Remember the conspiracy thing with Admiral Quinn and those parasites thirteen years back?"

Crewman Spiker grinned. "Before my time, Gramps."

"What isn't?" Hedrick grinned back. "Anyway, I heard 'bout that a week 'fore the press did."

"Fine, let me get this straight. The Romulans want to go to war, despite our being allies now, and are testing some new disabling weapon. Is that the latest from the Great and Powerful Mind of Randall Hedrick?"

Hedrick shrugged. "Maybe."

Leaning over and resting his arm on Hedrick's console, Spiker almost whispered, as if the two of them were keeping some dark secret. "Okay, Chief, one question: Why? Why now, and over what? We're all hurting from the Dominion War, the Romulans as much as us."

The older man shrugged. "I don't make the news, I just report it. Who knows why the people in charge do what they do? Five'll get you ten, even they don't know half the time."

Spiker cocked his head to one side, pursed his lips, then nodded. "Yeah, that one I buy."

Abruptly, Hedrick turned away toward a blinking monitor. "Hey, you picking this up?" Suddenly his accent was less defined.

Turning toward his own panel, Spiker punched up the same screen. "Yeah, got it. Priority report. Switching to speakers."

"This is Priority Channel from Starbase 10. We've lost all sensor and comm contact with the U.S.S. Dezago, eleven pars off Gamma Hydra Section two. Requesting search and support, Gamma Hydra, surrounding sectors. Starfleet, please respond."

Spiker shook his head. "Damn weak message. Lot of distortion."

"Not meant for us," Hedrick said. "I'm routing it to San Fran and Olympus Mons."

"Why Mars, too?"

"Buncha brass on Mars. You don't need to listen to barroom gossip, but you can at least read internal fleet memos. Brass meeting will wanna know."

"Yeah. Maybe this *is* something big."

Hedrick chuckled. "You're finally gettin' it, kid. And I reckon big won't even cast a shadow on this one."

Chapter Six

U.S.S. Enterprise, NCC-1701-E
Sector 001d
In orbit, Sol IV (Mars)

"THIS CAN'T BE RIGHT. Why would there be nuclear radiation?" Commander Will Riker handed the padd back
to the yeoman with a shake of his head. "Have Sciences
check their findings. I seriously doubt Mars has a nuclear pile somewhere."

Data turned from the ops station. "Actually, sir, I believe it does."

Pushing himself from the command chair, Riker took
a few steps forward as he motioned for the yeoman to
wait. "Come again, Mr. Data?"

Dabbing a few commands at his station before he

swiveled completely away from it, Data continued. "Dilithium re-crystallization experiments."

Looking back for a moment, Riker shared a glance with Deanna Troi, then turned his gaze back to Data. "That's possible?"

"Recently declassified Starfleet files, as well as contemporary experiments, have confirmed it, but I believe they are working on a less complicated method," Data said.

Riker let out a soft chuckle. "Learn something new every day."

"Indeed." As he turned back toward his console, Data nodded and his brows drew up.

"Question is, should we be registering anything from it?"

Data seemed to consider the question thoughtfully as he silently turned. "No. I do not believe that we should. Such radiation should be contained."

There was a feeling Riker sometimes got. Not so drastic as a sinking feeling in the stomach or his neck hair standing on end. This was just a little gut-twitch. Something that made his eyes squint a little, as if there was something to listen for that he couldn't quite hear.

Whether he ignored such feelings depended on the situation. This time, he didn't want to disregard it.

"Data, look into this."

"Aye, sir."

Riker turned away, stroking his currently beardless chin. "Captain wanted me to contact him if anything came up."

"Is something 'up' with this?" Deanna asked.

"Not sure." Riker lowered himself into the command chair. "But when the captain is in all-day meetings like this, a bad transporter circuit is big enough to interrupt him."

"Ah, of course." Deanna nodded and smiled that knowing smile.

"Then again," Riker added, returning her smile, "last time there were meetings to attend, he sent me and wouldn't do the same. We'll sit on this for a little longer."

Picard glanced at the timepiece to the left of the podium for the forty-third time. Admiral Dulroy, a.k.a. Admiral Dullard, had been talking for ninety-six minutes, the last fifty of which Picard had been praying the man would use some sort of punctuation. *My command for a comma,* he thought.

No such luck. Riker was to have called with something of false import at least thirty minutes ago. No luck there, either. Picard would see that his first officer suffered through a few Starfleet staff meetings himself.

Had the admirals that called the meeting been talking about the current HQ buzz, Picard would have been interested. The *Enterprise* had been the first to witness the dead zones in space. Since then, there'd been more such incidences. And well outside of the Romulan Neutral Zone. In fact, each such happening had been closer and closer to the heart of Federation space. It was possible Picard had been wrong about the Romulans not testing a weapon. And perhaps Picard had failed their test badly enough that the Romulans had decided to be increasingly bold. Of course, the nagging question was: why would they want to break a beneficial peace?

As Dulroy blanded his way through another volume of his speech, and Picard realized he'd not been listening for some time, finally the captain heard his communicator chirp.

He tapped it perhaps a bit too anxiously. "Picard here. Stand by." Rising, the captain bowed slightly, and whispered to those closest to him. "Urgent from my ship. Apologize to the admiralty for me."

One of the captains next to him nodded. Another chuckled lightly, probably wishing his first officer would make an urgent comm call about a bad batch of replicated coffee.

Once out in the hallway, Picard started a stride toward one of the HQ transporter rooms. "I'm hoping you have a good excuse for leaving me in there an extra hour, Number One."

"I do. We have a real alert situation, Captain."

That brought Picard up short for a moment. Then he quickened his gait. "Go."

"There's a nuclear reactor near Valles Marineris. It's heading for a . . . what did you call it, Data?"

"Meltdown, sir."

"Meltdown, Captain," Riker continued. *"No power to their coolant systems, no power of any kind. Only way we knew about it was they have a battery-powered backup comm system. It's on such a low frequency, the local authorities wouldn't even have heard it."*

"You've alerted Valles Marineris?"

"Aye, sir, but if power isn't restored, if enough pressure builds in the reactor core—"

"I understand. Beam down a—"

"Negative, sir, we can't beam into the complex. It's one of these dead zones—"

"Here?" On Mars. Hitting a bit too close to home now. "Alert Starfleet Command. And have Data and an engineering team take a runabout. They can beam me aboard on their way down."

"You're going with the team, sir?"

"Yes, Mr. Riker, I am. And if this weren't so important, I'd have you beam down here and continue the meetings in my stead. This time, you're lucky. Picard out."

S.S. Ralul
Sector 017c
In Orbit of Tellar V

"Commander, I swear, no mistake was made." Grono lowered his head and tensed himself for his boss's tirade.

"The mistakes you've made could not be counted by the most complex of computers, Grono!"

"Yes, sir."

"I don't know why I let you live."

"No, sir."

The commander grabbed the data tablet, looked at it a moment without seeming to actually read it, then tossed it back to Grono. "How can three freighters *and* their escorts be lost on a trade route they've traversed a million times?"

With the commander, such a question *could* be rhetorical. All Grono could do was wait to see if his silence was ignored or condemned.

"Well?" The commander barked. "Have you no input? Are you worth even a tenth of what I pay you?"

"I'm sorry, sir. I don't know what happened. There was a subspace message of power fluctuations in one of the haulers, and then silence from all three."

"That tells me what I know. You are to tell me what I don't know: *why?*"

When the commander's voice took such a tone, Grono often had to suppress a wince. This time he could not.

The commander noticed. "You are *useless!*"

"Sir, there are *some* rumors . . . other ships losing power and becoming disabled, even Starfleet vessels."

"Starfleet?" The commander straightened, shocked. "This must be very widespread, if Starfleet is involved." The commander turned away. "Send out my normal complaints to the Tellarite/Federation Liaison." He turned back quickly. "And I want you to contact the other trade ministers. I want to know who else has lost ships under these conditions."

Grono wrote that all down on the data padd. "Yes, sir." He wasn't sure how to react. His commander's tone seemed different from his other tirades.

"Something tells me that if this has happened to Starfleet's ships, it's more serious than a few lost freighters." The commander looked suddenly more calm, but also more tense. "I want to talk to Starfleet myself. I still have some friends there."

"Yourself, sir?"

Rather than admonishing Grono for questioning his superior, the commander was uncharacteristically solemn. "Yes. Contact Admiral Tarlan." He rose from his chair and turned toward the door. "I'll be in my quarters. Tell me when you have the admiral on the comm."

Enterprise Runabout *Hubble*
Sol IV (Mars)
Descending over Valles Marineris

"We have lost main power, sir."

"I can see that, Data." Picard watched the pilot struggle with the runabout controls more than should've been necessary. Had the research center been in the domed part of the city, there would have been no crosswind. As it was, with only thrusters for maneuvering, the ride was rough.

"We are still two kilometers from the research plant. Apparently, the area of the dead zone is increasing."

"I can see that, too, Data," Picard grumbled. "See if you can raise the station using nonsubspace frequencies."

"Aye, sir." Data turned away and Picard looked out the runabout's windows. Picard thought there was no sense in being guided completely by sensors that might cut out at any moment. And, perhaps it was old-fashioned, but something about flying in an atmosphere demanded a true bird's-eye view.

"No response, sir," Data said as he turned back toward Picard. The android looked out the window, down to his console, then out the windows again, following a point with his gaze as it passed out of view. Then he turned to the pilot. "Ensign, we are passing the landing pad."

"Ensign Sanderson is operating under my orders, Mr. Data," Picard said before the young man could defend himself to his superior officer. "The landing pad has a lift to the main building, and that lift might not be operational."

"But the dangers of landing so close to the building—"

"Won't matter if we don't get in there quickly and find a solution to the problem."

"Aye, sir."

One of the oddities about Data, Picard thought, was that, unless he was in decision-mode, he didn't think like a commander, he thought like one of the commanded, and so he thought mostly about rules, and not when it was a good time to break such rules. Picard had seen Data in command, and found him to be quite good, but when Picard was in charge, Data always seemed a bit different, his mind in a different thought pattern. Not the most severe of problems, and Data wasn't insubordinate. He just asked bothersome questions at times.

Of course, Picard could order Data not to do so, but the one time he had, Picard found the android too quiet, too sterile. It was Data's personality to be the way he was, and Picard liked him. As with all those one calls friends, one understands the balance that is toleration.

A wind gust suddenly turned the runabout's bow away from the research reactor, and Sanderson had to turn into the gale before trying to zigzag back on course. As slowly as possible with the sudden down current Picard felt on the hull, the runabout landed on the sidewalk near the main entrance. It was part of the terraformed but rough Mars terrain, no space suits were necessary, but out of doors the atmosphere was on the thin side, the temperature on the cold side, and the gravity on the light side.

Picard, Data, Gibson, and a crew of six engineers spilled quickly out of the runabout and through the main doors. Once the outer doors closed behind them, the inner set parted way.

"You're from Starfleet?" A tall man greeted them, somewhat relieved, somewhat weary.

"Picard, from *Enterprise*. We have a crew to assist—"

The man shook his head. He looked old and tired, his eyes sunken, his hair a mess of blond and gray. "No, there is nothing to do. Leave, and take my staff with you. Everyone else has evacuated."

With a wave of his hand, Picard ordered his team forward. "Data, find the main control room. Sanderson, gather any nonessential personnel and see them to the runabout." His men left quickly to carry out their orders, and the captain turned to face the man who'd warned them all away. "Who are you?"

"La Croix. I'm the project director," he said. "I appreciate you want to help, but . . ." The man had obviously been up all night, and as Picard began walking past him, La Croix seemed almost too tired to follow. "There's nothing to be done. I've tried everything, thought of everything. Our containment systems are off-line. Pressure has caused a partial fuel meltdown and the coolant lines are closed off. Do you understand what that means?"

At first Picard thought he might moderate his gait to accommodate the director, but he decided to pick up his pace toward what signs had told him was the station control room. "I understand, Mr. La Croix. I'm familiar with the technology, and I understand why these things happened a few hundred years back, but today?"

The door to the control center opening too slowly for him, Picard stepped sideways and pushed through before the panel was completely out of his way.

La Croix followed. "You don't understand. It shouldn't have happened 'today.' We had fail-safe upon fail-safe, but we expected containment fields to be working. They won't. We can't explain it but—"

"But only batteries are working, and those don't have enough power, correct?"

Surprised, La Croix stopped walking as Picard marched toward Data. "Ah . . . yes, correct."

"Data?" the captain prompted.

The android turned away from the console, a bit more slowly than it seemed he should have. Picard had to remind himself that within these dead-power zones Data wasn't at his most efficient. "The situation is grave, sir. There is very little time before the pressure builds to a point where the outer seals will crack, contaminating the atmosphere. Most of Valles Marineris is domed, but some parts are not. . . ."

His shoulders stooped, La Croix looked down sadly. "This just shouldn't be. The chances of this happening were seven billion to one."

Picard glanced up at Data.

"He is very close, sir."

"Mr. La Croix, it *has* happened," Picard said, "so now we must deal with it. Is there any way to seal this off, contain the pressure?"

The android shook his head, as did La Croix, but only Data spoke. "Not in time, except with a containment field, but the batteries available would last but a few moments."

"The *Enterprise* could swing into a low orbit, generate a containment field . . ."

"Yes, sir, but not for very long, at that range and of this size. If we could even form one in this dead-power zone. As you remember, using our tractor beams—"

"Tractor beams."

"Sir?"

"Data, how long before we lose containment?"

"Difficult to say exactly, without proper sensor readings. The dead zone hampers our more advanced sensors, and the radiation hampers the lower-technology scanners. Without proper study—"

"Guess, Data," Picard barked.

"Fifteen minutes, sir," Data said quickly. Then he added, "Give or take."

Picard allowed himself the briefest of smiles. "Let's hope that's enough. Evacuate all personnel from the center. And I mean every last person." He turned to La Croix. "How many people would that be?"

It took a moment for La Croix to answer, as if he was thinking of each person in turn, remembering where they were, then taking mental note of it. "Ten—no, eleven, including myself."

"Plenty of time," Picard said as he took La Croix's shoulder and guided him quickly toward the door.

"What? Plenty of time for what? There's nothing that can be done."

"From here?" Picard said, "No. From the *Enterprise*, a great deal."

"Sir, you're breaking up badly." Squinting, straining to hear through bursts of static, Riker twisted toward Shapiro at ops. "Boost the gain on that."

"There's . . . a lot . . . time. I need beams . . . station as soon as out of . . . ange."

Frustrated, Riker shook his head and stomped from the command chair. "Ensign—"

"I'm trying, sir." The young man's hands danced over the ops console a bit nervously. "Here we go."

"Enterprise, do you read?"

"We do now, Captain. Repeat your last message."

"I want all available nonessential power diverted to tractor beams. We have to punch through that dead zone and we have less than five minutes to do it."

"Sir?" Riker leaned over to see the ops station's sensor console. "I have you just coming out of the dead zone. Why would we need to tractor you?"

"Not us, Number One. The entire reactor."

Enterprise's powerful tractor beam sliced through atmosphere, energy, raw and determined, dancing in the thin Martian air as it pulled on the red planet itself, tore a chunk of crust from the surface. And with it, the hemorrhaging nuclear reactor.

From the *Hubble,* the scene was rather blissful for a moment, then it lurched out of Picard's view. The control consoles dimmed and the runabout dipped awkwardly and too quickly. He struggled with the controls as the wind thrashed the runabout up and to the side, then down and around. Picard felt his chair fall from under him as the ship lost altitude. He turned to Data and found the android giving a very human shake of his head, as if trying to clear mental cobwebs, or rattle off a stunning blow.

"Transfer shield power to impulse drive," Picard ordered.

"Impulse is off-line," Sanderson said, his voice tinged with minor panic.

Data's voice was tight with apprehension. "I am weakened myself, sir. The dead zone has expanded."

It had never done that before, at least not that they'd recorded. How, why, and all the other nagging questions simmered in the back of Picard's mind as he gazed at Sanderson's console. The ensign was trying to pilot a rock through a tornado. It was a very lost cause. Backup batteries wouldn't provide enough lift and everything else was off-line. The runabout was falling quickly from the Martian sky.

"Picard to *Enterprise.*"

"*We're scanning you, Captain,*" Riker said. "*See your situation. Trying to get a transporter lock now.*"

The captain glanced at Data. If applied right, the thrusters might at least level their descent as they fell. Might. Runabouts weren't gliders meant to ride air currents, they were powerhouses. They used energy to bend physics into the control of man. Without power, there was no control.

"I am unable to determine where the dead zone ends, sir," Data said. "If we could maneuver out of it—"

"Assume we can't. Can we help *Enterprise* get a transporter lock?"

Data's expression seemed blank for a moment, as if lost in thought. It wasn't something Picard was used to seeing on him. "If we transfer all power to our transporter, it may provide a signal on which to lock. Both signals in conjunction may be able to break through the dead zone."

"Make it so."

The android nodded hastily and began his task. Sanderson set his board to transfer power as well, after locking thrusters on a course up and away from any possible settlements. If the runabout was going to crash, it would have a lot of wilderness in which to do it.

"Did you get all that, Number One? Can you link into our pad?"

"Got it, Captain. Data's fed us the coordinates. Ready when you are."

Darting from his seat, Data went into the small transporter alcove and began moving isolinear chips in and out of a control unit. "We will only be able to transport two at a time."

Picard nodded. "Begin with the reactor personnel."

"This is safe?" one of the scientists' voices cracked as Data ushered him onto one of the two transporter pads.

"Safer than crashing, sir," Data said, and Picard

couldn't help but allow himself the briefest of smiles. Out of the mouths of androids . . .

"We're ready with the first two, Number One," Picard said. They were plummetting like a stone now, and seeming weightlessness was taking over.

"Energizing."

A shower of light and sparkle fell over two very tense-looking scientists. The process lasted longer than it should. The two men didn't dematerialize for a few moments, and then finally the process ended, taking them with it, up into orbit.

"Rough ride, but we have the first two, sir," Riker said. *"We'd better hurry."*

Two by two Data led the scientists into the transporter alcove, then the engineering personnel. *Picard's Ark,* the captain thought with a smile. Each beam-out took only seconds, but it seemed quite long for a transport, especially when riding a wind-torn runabout up and down as it fell, lifted a bit with a gust of air, only to fall farther on the next downturn.

"Thrusters are gone," Sanderson said as he got up and joined the last engineer on the transporter pad. "I've slowed descent, but it'll pick up again fast now."

As the pair dematerialized, Riker's voice said, *"Reactor plant is out of the atmosphere and pushed out of orbit, Captain. We're experiencing power drains. Interference from those dead zones. Better hurry."*

Picard hesitated a brief moment. He was leaving this vessel, an extension of his starship, to crash in the wilderness of a barren planet. He touched the chair's headrest a moment more, then nodded to Data. "Forty seconds before she crashes."

"Aye, sir." Data set the controls as the captain stepped onto the left pad, then he got onto the right pad himself. "Energize."

A feeling of desperation washed over Picard as he looked out into the runabout and waited for the transporter to work. He was on a crashing ship, and doing nothing to stop it from happening. There *was* nothing to do, and he knew that, but . . . his instincts told him to try, not merely to stand and wait for rescue.

"Captain, we're . . . prob . . . can't . . . lo . . ." Riker's voice deteriorated into comm static. Picard had the urge to step forward, off the transporter pad. He kept himself from doing so. *Enterprise* would still be trying to beam them off, even if they were having communications trouble.

"Sir," the captain heard Data say, "if they cannot beam us—"

But that was all Data had a chance to say. The universe crunched darkness and pain around Picard, and silence blanketed all.

Chapter Seven

"WE'VE LOST THE TRANSPORTER SIGNAL!"

Riker stomped toward the ops console. "I don't want to hear that. Get it back!"

"No use, Commander. It's gone."

He jabbed at his comm badge. "Transporter room, report!"

"Never got a clear lock, sir!"

Tapping at the console, Riker ordered the ops officer: "Plot trajectory from last known course and position. I want them found *now!*"

"Wait, I'm picking up a beacon from the surface of the planet. Coming from a debris field."

"Get a damned lock."

"Aye, sir. Trying."

* * *

Sound came first, undefined and wavering, like a soft rustling of paper or linen. Light danced in his head, and as he pulled himself from a bleak dream of nothingness, Picard heard Data telling him not to move.

The android's voice sounded quiet in the thin Martian atmosphere. Picard wondered just how great his pain would have been with one Earth G crushing down on him instead of the lighter gravity of Mars. With that wandering thought of pain came the flood of agony, first in sharp needle-pricks, then in hammers, and he gasped as Data removed a piece of wreckage that had sliced into the captain's leg.

"I am sorry, sir. That was necessary to free you."

"Quite . . ." Picard grunted as he tried to get up, and failed. ". . . all right, Mr. Data. I seem to have broken a leg, and perhaps my arm."

Data ran a medical tricorder scanner over his captain. "Yes, sir. And you are bleeding in three places."

"Mm-hmm." Picard tried to brace himself with his good arm on the wall of the transporter alcove. He couldn't do that either. He wasn't even sure where he would have gone if he could.

The runabout was mostly intact, except for some very large cracks. The cold wind poured through those, and actually felt rather good. It wouldn't in a few minutes, when Picard's body was out of shock from the crash, but for now . . .

"I suggest you not move, sir. I have a medikit. Let me stop the bleeding."

Picard nodded. "Are you injured?"

"I am not damaged, and we appear to be either out

of, or at least on the edge of, the dead zone, some two-hundred-and-seventy kilometers outside Valles Marineris."

"How do you know we're out of the dead zone?"

"I am feeling much better, sir."

"Glad to hear it." His right arm too painful to move, Picard tapped his comm badge awkwardly with his left. "Picard to—"

The captain stopped, turning his neck painfully toward the din of a transporter beam materialization. Riker, Dr. Crusher, and two people from security appeared a few feet to Picard's left.

Almost before she'd fully beamed, Crusher was already plunging toward the captain. She ran her tricorder quickly over his body. "Hairline fractures in your right leg, multiple lacerations, abrasions, contusions . . . and a clean break in your arm. No wonder you hate these meetings with the admiralty."

Picard nodded. "Indeed. And it's going to get worse. Do what you have to do to get me mobile again, Doctor. I need to speak to the lot of them immediately."

"Captain, th-that's a closed door meeting," the young yeoman stammered. Obviously he didn't like having to yell at a starship captain.

"I'm opening it." Still a bit stiff, Picard limped quickly through the doorway as the entryway parted before him.

Seven admirals looked toward him simultaneously. He continued across the room until he was at their conference table. Hovering in the middle of the table was a holographic representation of the Alpha Quadrant. White blotches dotted the three-dimensional graph. What they represented, Picard could guess.

"Dead zones," he said.

Dulroy, Picard noticed, was nowhere to be seen. In this room were the heads of Starfleet, those who were really in charge. Admiral Tucker motioned Picard to a chair. "Have a seat, Picard."

Tucker was the most senior member of the fleet and the head of the Joint Chiefs of Staff to the Federation president. Venerable, unpliable, a bit of a jackass to people he didn't like and didn't like him. But those were a misguided few. Picard didn't know him much better than knowing all of that, but he liked the admiral nevertheless.

"We have a very big problem," Tucker said.

"I know." Picard's tone was grave and a bit rough, in part because his bones were only freshly healed and his muscles still quite sore.

The admiral shook his gray head. "You don't know everything. Three hours ago we received information that, two days previous, a shipment of antimatter had been lost, presumed destroyed. This shipment had been transferred from a Federation government freighter to a Romulan one. It was a replacement for materials leased from the Romulans in the Dominion War."

"Lost?" Picard asked. "How?"

Shaking his head and indulging in a sigh, Tucker leaned forward against the table. "We don't know. We assume it's these dead zones, but we're not sure. And what's more, the Romulans aren't sure. Since their freighter never returned, they're beginning to assume the worst. As are the Klingons. They've lost twelve ships, that they know of."

"The Klingons know about the dead zones," Picard said.

"Yes, but every government is suspecting that every other government is causing them." Tucker looked tired. Worried. "What's worse, we can't even discuss it with them. Subspace communications are all but totally useless now." He tapped on the computer padd on the table and the holograph before them twisted into a network of communication lines that disappeared into the white blotches previously shown. "Everywhere a signal falls into a dead zone, it's lost. But knowing that's the reason is little comfort. What's the first thing an enemy does before invasion?"

"Jams or destroys communications, of course. But why now? I doubt—"

"So do I. I don't think the Romulans, the Klingons, the Breen, whoever are launching an invasion. The major Alpha Quadrant powers are too weak right now . . . but others? Those who might take advantage of our collective weakness, perhaps? I don't know."

"I came here because I know what a threat these dead zones are. I respectfully request permission that the *Enterprise* be assigned."

Tucker waved off the request. "I appreciate that, Captain, but no, I need *Enterprise* in the Romulan Neutral Zone. Covertly."

"Covertly?" Picard's brow furrowed. "Things have

broken down between the Federation and the Romulans that quickly." It wasn't a question.

"With all the ships being lost, only Ambassador Worf and Chancellor Martok are keeping the Klingons with us right now. We've managed to get through to Worf on taD, and we've got envoys en route to all the other major governments. But without subspace radio, a message only travels as fast as the ship that carries it."

It all sounded very ominous, Picard thought. "Why do you need *Enterprise* in the Neutral Zone?"

"It's not a why," Tucker said as he keyed into his padd again. This time the holograph became a person, not a starmap. "It's a who."

Picard's muscles tensed and his own breath felt heavy. "Spock."

Chapter Eight

Planetary Defense Station
Merterbis Colony
Romulan Empire

Five days ago

"YOU TOLD ME AN HOUR AGO you'd have that circuit replaced, didn't you? Is my faith in you misplaced?" Folan was snapping at her assistant, and she wished she could take the edge from her tone, but she couldn't. She tried to remind herself it wasn't as if her mere demand could change the speed at which physics insisted a task be finished. Her people were good, and she knew better.

Then again, so did her team. They probably knew the tension in Folan's voice was only a fraction of that which stiffened her shoulders and neck. The most important moment of her life, and T'sart would be on hand to see it. Who was she kidding? He was not here just to watch, but to critique her every move. Once a teacher, always a teacher. And she, always the student.

At least T'sart had some level of admiration for her abilities. Her commander, J'emery, did not. He'd taken the accolades for saving his ship from a power desert when so many others had been lost. As if it was his accomplishment and not hers. She'd saved the lives of the crew, a crew from which only she had risked her life and career to stop their idiot commander from killing them all. Only Picard had seemed to sense that Folan had made some special effort, and reading an alien was difficult, so her notion could be quite wrong. For all she knew, he merely had eaten a lunch that disagreed with him that day.

She needed to focus, she reminded herself. It was not good to let her mind spin about on such things she could not change. If only she didn't feel so rushed . . .

T'sart himself had moved up the timeline for her tests, claiming that if this worked they might have at least some defense against any attack force. Attack forces were all the Senate was talking about, with the subspace communication problems and the lost vessels. Her people were suspicious by nature, but Folan was usually not. The tense times, however . . . She chastised herself for thinking the worst. She was a scientist. She was not supposed to fear that which she didn't understand. She was supposed to do what she must to understand it.

A brown slice of hair fell from behind her ear and, frustrated, she pushed it back in place. T'sart was looking at her, she could tell. Those cool eyes on her from behind the monitoring station he'd wandered to. It was Folan he monitored, not the experiment.

"It goes well," she told him across the console room. She knew there were other people about, but she saw only T'sart. Only he was important to her right now.

He smiled that thin smile that she'd never been quite able to read. "All things *seem* in order," he said.

Folan made her way toward him, checking the computer monitors at other stations as she went. She despised someone looking over her shoulder as she worked, but couldn't resist doing it to others. Especially in this case.

She'd risked her reputation on this idea. Scientists were not always given high esteem in the Senate, and while they had their voice there, it was often not heard.

But the concept was elegant, she thought, and thanks to T'sart's support among his Senate allies, she'd pushed it through.

All scientists had plans and ideas, "notions and potions," as T'sart would sometimes say. Folan was no different. Yet rarely did she have an idea she considered graceful, one that seemed like some marble construction in her head, whereas other concepts were but stacks of neatly arranged but unsightly twigs in comparison.

And if it worked, if a large planetary power plant could provide energy to an orbiting ship defending the planet directly and without a prohibitive power loss . . . Folan would have her start on a reputation that could rival T'sart's.

Folan was as tall as her teacher, but she'd always

looked up to him, and still, when she came close to him, she felt as if she were glancing up at an angle.

"I believe we are ready to start," she said, hoping her nervousness did not reverberate through her voice. "Would you like to join me at the main sensor console?"

T'sart nodded pleasantly. "Of course. I'm a bit surprised we're not monitoring this from your vessel. Any problems won't be from the power plant sending the power, but on the vessels in orbit that are attempting to receive it."

"Well . . . I've not cleared that with Commander J'emery, and he's in meetings with the colony governor. He specifically asked not to be disturbed."

With a smile that could power its own starship, T'sart leaned down and whispered. "Your commander is in conference with a local prostitute. He's right here, on this installation, in a room specially prepared for his indiscretion. Most of your ship's senior officers are partaking of similar indulgences. If you were truly more than a pawn in life, not only would you be aware of this, you'd make sure you had a holographic recording of it. One prospers in life by seizing control of destiny and commanding it. Opportunity will not court with the truly gifted—we must rape it."

"I—" Folan froze for a moment. Was it a joke? Was she to laugh? Had he lost his mind? Why would he say such a thing, even in a hushed tone, where people could hear or his voice could itself be recorded?

"In any case, your commander *did* say not to disturb him. But this is your project, and your experiment.

Surely you can make this decision on your own." T'sart continued that odd smile, friendly and yet mirthless.

"Yes," Folan said slowly, hesitant to disagree with him, if only because she wouldn't be able to guess his next reaction. "I suppose I can."

U.S.S. Enterprise, NCC 1701-E
Romulan Neutral Zone
Section 74

Picard paced, and he didn't indulge in that often. He was on his starship, in his ready room, perhaps the only place he truly felt completely comfortable, and yet . . . this was not where he wanted to be.

"Captain?"

He'd not spoken to Deanna Troi much since she'd entered. She'd respected his silence until now.

"Please don't tell me what I'm feeling," he said finally, deciding to stop and peer out the window.

"You know me better than that," she said. "As an empath I dropped the 'I know how you feel' line a long time ago. I'm here because you invited me in to talk. So, with all due respect, Captain, talk."

Turning toward her, the slightest of smiles tugging up his frown, he nodded and sighed quietly. "I'm frustrated. I walk in to speak with the admiralty to demand one assignment, and I limp out with another."

"They're putting a lot of resources on it now, and notifying all—"

"Maybe too little, too late. There's something

more to these dead zones than even Starfleet is admitting."

"To you?"

"To themselves."

"How is that?"

He paused, standing silent a moment, trying to find an apt description. "That's just it, I'm not sure. I don't normally feel like disobeying direct orders based on a gut feeling."

"You're disobeying orders—"

"I *feel* like it. But, no, I'm here. Treading through the Romulan Neutral Zone without permission—when by all rights we should be able to get that permission."

"I'd heard the Romulans pulled their ambassadors from the Council."

Picard nodded. "Yes, and haven't been seen since. They're presumed lost by the Federation. Who knows what the Romulans are assuming? Subspace communications are working with less and less frequency and reliability. None of the major governments can talk with any alacrity. The war's been over less than three months, and already the peace is falling apart."

Deanna sat silently a moment. "Do you really think this message Starfleet received was from Spock?"

"If it was, I agree we need to be where he requested we be. If it's not, then I suppose we need to find out what has happened to him. Assuming the worst, whoever used Spock's Starfleet codes would have needed to get them from Spock." Picard paused. He heard his voice soften. "If that's the case . . . it's not good."

"If it *is* Spock," she said, "perhaps it's the first real sign of Vulcan humor rearing its head."

He smiled, then caught himself and pursed his lips.

Deanna leaned forward. "You don't want to smile." It wasn't a question.

He thought on that for a moment anyway, then decided, "No. How can I smile? We might have lost a Starfleet legend . . . and we can't even depend on space itself anymore. Any other time I'd want to be the one leading this mission . . . but right now, this . . . these dead zones . . . there's something unnatural about them. That's the mystery I want to see through. Not whether or not this is a trap."

Deanna nodded lightly. "But if Spock's presence has been compromised and he was captured—"

"They wouldn't be able to get information out of him," Picard said gravely. "They'd kill him."

**Romulan Warbird *Makluan*
In Orbit, Merterbis colony
Romulan Empire**

Folan watched as delicate threads of power, invisible to the naked eye but given shape and form by computer enhancement, unraveled from the planet below. On each of five monitors, one warbird apiece, the energy beam connected.

"Impressive, is it not?" Folan asked of T'sart. Too enveloped in her own satisfaction to keep the pride from her voice, she smiled and watched, as if a triumphant general who'd won the final battle of the final war for all eternity.

She glanced back at T'sart. He seemed to look her way only at moments their gazes met, though she was not certain of this. His was an enigmatic visage ofttimes, and today was no different. As his student, Folan had frequently searched his dark eyes for a hint of regard for his student. And occasionally he had some. But it never seemed enough.

"Yes," T'sart said, and tilted his head into a nod. "This day has been well-planned."

He smiled, and at first that elated her, and then she felt its coolness descend over her like a thick, suffocating fog.

Folan nodded back. "Thank you," she murmured, and felt her brow furrow just the slightest bit. As he turned toward a console, probably to check some sensor readouts, she turned slowly back to watch the bridge's main viewscreen. "Initiate the combat tests."

The centurion nodded, and issued the order to the other vessels.

On the tactical display, a row of the Praetor's finest warbirds swooped down to attack the lead vessel. A vessel that now received its power directly from the planet below. They all did.

This was the future of planetary defense, Folan thought as disruptors pounded into shields that wouldn't weaken. She was the architect of that future, and she alone.

One pursuit at which her people excelled was the art of war. The games they played today were with full weapons at point-blank range . . . and Folan's power transfers were holding up. As if each vessel had the defensive—and offensive—power output of an entire planet.

Already she was considering upgrading the computer subsystems to help reduce a power fluctuation she saw on one monitor a few moments ago. At the same time, Folan was imagining her speech in the Senate as she accepted the Praetor's Military Excellence Award, a decoration that T'sart had been the only scientist yet to receive. As well, she was planning to research the possibilities of creating a power network that would protect not just a planet, but an entire solar system.

If that was even necessary. This feat alone should be enough to make Folan's life a boon. From this point forward, any planet the Praetor chose to defend would be impervious to attack. Taking a planet into the Empire would mean keeping it. Ground would be gained, and never lost, so long as there were planetary power plants to feed the battleships above. Enemies would fire, and shields would not fall. Disruptors would strike, and never lose their bite. The possibilities—and her future—seemed limitless.

And then it all toppled.

The lead vessel, the *P'tarch,* suddenly pitched to one side, her shields bubbling with energy. Electrical fire crackled back and forth in waves that rolled over one another.

She had not been fired upon. Something was wrong.

The centurion at the helm turned toward Folan. "Power overload on the *P'tarch.*"

"Discontinue energy extraction!"

"Overrides are not working, Sub-Commander!"

The display monitors flashed overlapping problems. All that could go wrong, had.

Folan hunched over her interface to the main computer. She gave commands and cross commands. She tried the most basic of contingencies, and the most outrageous. Many of them should have worked. Some of them didn't have a chance. None of them helped. Panic filled her lungs as if she was drowning. She gasped for an answer.

For a brief moment, she looked back to T'sart. Seeking advice. Perhaps his counsel held a solution, an inkling of an idea. A hint. Anything.

He stood tall in the thunder that was the bridge, an experiment in chaos. Of course he stood tall and unmoving. He was her teacher, and always would be. Within her, she almost wished he would admit this was a simulation and that, while she had failed, she could take the test again.

All too real, and perhaps almost with surreality, he did not answer her pleaful gaze. All he did was glance back, and then finally say: "Even the unplanned is planned by all our actions."

A flash of light pulled her back toward the main bridge viewscreen.

On the display, the *P'tarch* seemed to arch its hull in an explosion. It began a steep fall toward the planet, and was quickly lost in a ball of fire.

Another ship had sped toward the first, attempting a tractor beam. That failed, and yet a third ship joined when it was too late.

"The other ships!" Folan screamed, as the easy

threads of energy that connected them with the planet became thick bars of power. Rolling and shuddering with electrical flame, each vessel ruptured and split. Two singular explosions from within two bright starflashes, that were gone as quickly as they'd come.

Their debris spread out, some into the planet's atmosphere, some toward the *Makluan* and in all directions.

"Shields!" Folan said with too much hesitation. She'd forgotten that not only was she in command of the experiment, but in command of the ship as well. She didn't want that. She wanted to deflect command to someone else. With most of the ship's officers planetside, and the rest under her authority for this project . . . there was no one to whom she could surrender control.

Except T'sart.

Folan turned again to the aft bridge. He was the ranking officer—

And he was also gone.

She spun around, stumbling from her seat.

"Sub-Commander!" the centurion called. "Your orders?"

She pivoted back, saw the large spread of debris that rushed toward the main viewer. "Evasive," she roared. "Full deflectors!"

Another order given too late, she thought, by someone not practiced enough to give it.

Metal crunched through the shields, and then against the hull.

Darkness followed a flash of light, and smoke filled her lungs.

Folan's future was no more.

Chapter Nine

U.S.S. Defiant, NX-74205
Federation Sector 46
Near the Bajoran System

"DEFI . . . COME IN! WE'VE ALL MAIN . . . wer. Do not . . . Do y . . . read?"

Commander Tiris Jast turned toward Lieutenant Nog at ops. "That barely even sounded like Colonel Kira. What's wrong with the signal?"

Nog shrugged nervously and sounded overly excited. "I—I don't know. Something's wrong with the signal at its origin." Nog had often been nervous in Jast's presence. Strange, since Ferengi and Bolian had worked together before with some success.

"Calm yourself, Lieutenant," she said. "Try to raise Deep Space Nine again."

"Yes, ma'am."

The turbolift doors parted, and Dr. Julian Bashir strode onto the bridge. "Are we having a problem with communications? I was downloading something from the station database and suddenly lost my datalink."

"It may be related," Jast said, then held up her blue hand to stop the doctor from further utterance. "Helm, set a course back to the station," she ordered.

Bashir waited a long moment, then finally asked, "May I speak now?"

She thought his tone might have been somewhat annoyed. If so, he was too easily irritated. "Yes."

"If there's a problem at the station, perhaps we shouldn't just change our course, but increase our speed?"

Jast turned toward him fully by swiveling the command chair. "By the time I finish explaining this to you, we will be fifty-three seconds from minimum scanning range of the station. Before making any tactical decisions, I must know the facts of the situation. I know two facts—that we've lost contact with the station, and they were trying to order us *not* to do something. That could have been, 'Do not return to port.'"

Bashir sighed. "And if I don't reply at all, thereby ending this discussion, when will we be within scanner range?"

"There is no discussion. I explained my position, and expected you to disagree, but I didn't intend to debate it further. We will now be within scanner range in forty seconds."

The doctor shook his head and sat down at one of the bridge science stations. "Aye, aye, sir," he said.

"Lieutenant, scan the station," Jast ordered when enough time had elapsed.

"Scanning . . ." Nog bent over one of his sensor consoles. "Readings are faint, Commander. Null power output from the main reactors. I am reading battery power active."

"Signs of other vessels?"

Nog hesitated as he pored over the screens. His voice was calm now, but soaked in perplexity. "Same vessels as when we left port," he said. "But I know that two freighters were scheduled to leave half an hour ago, and they're still on Upper Pylons 2 and 3."

"Slow to impulse power."

The conn officer nodded and tapped at her controls. "Aye."

Bashir leaned toward the command chair. "Now we're slowing?"

"Do you have any idea what's going on, Doctor?" Jast continued to look from the forward viewer to one of her own command chair screen readouts.

Seeming taken aback by the question, Bashir hesitated. "No. I don't. But I'd like to find out."

"As would I," she said. "But rushing into what could be harm's way, when Colonel Kira was likely warning us away, would be inadvisable."

"Of course," Bashir said. "You're right. I'm sorry."

Jast gave him a slight smile. "It's—I understand."

They both nodded at one another, and then Jast turned toward Nog. "Continue scans as we approach."

"Aye—" Nog stopped in mid-sentence and mid-jab on his console. "Wait, what's wrong?"

The normal hum of the *Defiant*'s systems slowed and then stopped. Lights clicked off for just a second before emergency lights flashed on.

"Report."

"Impulse power is gone." Nog slammed commands into his console, but to no avail. "So is warp. We've lost main power."

"Jast to Engineering."

There was no reply.

She tapped her comm badge. "Engineering, this is the bridge." Silence, and Jast didn't try again. "Sensors?"

"Trying to re-calibrate now, Commander," Nog said.

"And try to raise Starfleet Command. Something is very wrong here."

Station Deep Space Nine
Federation Sector 47
Bajoran system

"We don't *know* what's wrong, Quark." Kira jabbed at her desktop computer screen but didn't look up at the Ferengi who refused to leave her office. "If we knew, we'd fix it."

"In the meantime," the Ferengi asked, "can we at least put the Promenade back on battery power?"

Kira growled. "No."

"How do you expect me to run a bar without power for replicators or holosuites or even the dabo wheel?"

Kira sighed. "Quark, I'm unimpressed. We both know you're not this stupid."

"Excuse me?"

"Oh, granted, I've had my doubts in the past," she mumbled to herself.

"What are you talking about?" Quark looked almost wounded.

"You don't think for a minute I'd take battery power away from docking clamps and life support. You're just here to learn what you can about what's going on. I commend you, really, I do, but . . ." She looked up at him and raised her voice. "I don't *know* what's going on. Get it?"

Now Quark smiled. "Got it."

She nodded. "Then get out."

Chapter Ten

**Romulan Warbird *Makluan*
Decaying orbit around Merterbis
   colony
Romulan Empire**

FOLAN TRIED TO LATCH onto the normal sounds that
would tell her she was still on the bridge. She couldn't.
The din of destruction crashed down on her. Little
could be made out of the chaos that was her vessel ex-
ploding around her.

She felt no pain, and feared her neck or spine had
snapped. A moment later she was sorry that wasn't the
case. Pulling herself slowly back into the command
chair was an adventure in agony. Every muscle was
tight with strain, and her head pounded as she tried to

sort out the cacophony of sound that was her ship struggling for life.

"S-status." She sputtered the order and felt the command seat under her, but it gave her physical, not mental support. Should she be here? She was a science officer, not command grade.

Medric, the ship's fourth officer, answered from one of the engineering stations. "All main systems are off-line. We've sustained a great deal of internal damage in the engineering decks. Sensors are off-line, but a last burst of data reported a chain reaction within the orbiting vessels and every power plant on the planet. Explosions from overloads seem to be massive, and expanding."

Focusing on what she thought Commander J'emery would have ordered, Folan turned toward Medric and croaked out commands. "Try to raise the planet and contact the commander. Contact anyone. We have to know for sure what's going on, and stop it if we can."

"How did this happen?" Medric asked, his tone sharp with accusation.

"I—" Folan began an answer, but caught herself. She didn't have to answer to him. He was command and she was science, but he was still a subordinate, and as the rest of the bridge crew looked between them to see what her answer would be, she knew there could be none. "I gave you an order," Folan said. "Follow it."

Medric glared, perhaps measuring the situation, perhaps measuring Folan's will to command. She *could* turn control of the vessel to him. There was a provision for that in the regulations. It was an easy matter. It was much more difficult for him to wrest that command from her. Difficult, but not impossible.

After what seemed like too long a moment, Medric nodded his acceptance and silently went about his task.

Around her, for the first time Folan felt how the bridge must have to J'emery when he was in command. Yes, the ship was in disarray. But it was hers. She was in command, and while her career might be over as soon as they returned home, for now she was in charge and in control of her own destiny.

Medric's question crackled in her mind's ear. *How did this happen?* To that, Folan added another question as she looked toward the science station, her usual console. *Where is T'sart?*

Without sensors there would be little data that would be of use to Folan. But T'sart's absence was a tangible mystery she *could* solve. And he, perhaps, might know how to stop the chain reaction that was destroying the power plants on the planet.

"Computer, where is Commander T'sart?"

The computer replied: *"Commander T'sart is in corridor three-three."*

There must have been some mistake, Folan thought. She'd misheard. Why would he be in—

She shook the thought from her head. It didn't matter. Perhaps under his bluster and brilliance and arrogance T'sart was, at heart, a coward. She needed him and, whatever his state of mind, she needed his experience and knowledge. He had looked over her program protocols for the power plant distribution net. He might know what could now be causing a cascading overload.

Folan lurched toward the turbolift, then stalled before the opening door. A moment of indecision: should she leave the bridge in the command of another as she found T'sart?

Medric asked the question as well. "Is the Sub-Commander relinquishing the bridge?"

She pivoted toward him on the heel of her boot. "Negative. Your sub-commander is leaving the bridge for a moment. But *I* am in command. You will signal me if there is *any* change in status."

"Yes, Sub-Commander."

She stared at Medric a moment, then escaped into the lift.

A layer of smoke and mist laced the corridor. Folan did not see T'sart, and when she called up the computer again to check his location, only static responded.

She thought about searching the few rooms on this end of the hall, but before she could take action, she felt the pressure of a weapon in her back, and heard the rasp of his voice.

"Don't move."

At his command, Folan turned slowly. A million possibilities flooding her mind, shocking her. A mistake, she thought. She always blamed herself first. She'd somehow stumbled into a Tal Shiar plot, or . . .

No. Nothing made sense.

"I suppose I miscalculated," T'sart said as he motioned her toward a doorway. A transporter room. "I was certain you'd be either panicking or in the midst of turmoil about your experiment."

"I—" She began to say something, she wasn't even sure what, but he shook his head and whispered for her to move. He punctuated the command with a jerking motion of his disruptor.

It was an odd sight to Folan. She thought many things of T'sart, but a thug was not one of them. And he was acting like a thug.

"I don't understand," she said as she entered the room. She was a bit embarrassed. Her voice sounded young, almost childish, even to herself. T'sart must have thought worse: he laughed.

He gestured toward the empty center of the room. "Stand there." She followed the request—the order, the threat, really—and felt her upper lip sweating. Had T'sart lost his mind? Was there a coup? Was he leading a coup? Was he running from one?

"I'd kill you personally," he said as he fussed with the transporter console, "but if I really thought *you* a threat, you'd already be dead."

Folan said nothing. She simply stared in silence as he set the disruptor down on the panel so that he could use both hands to configure what was presumably his escape.

Escape, yes but why? He had little to lose, because her experiment was a failure. Hers was the career that was ruined.

"This makes no sense," she said finally.

"To you? I'm sure it doesn't. You've always been one of my slower-witted students."

She felt her brow knit, then her face flushed with anger.

He looked up, obviously noticed, and so qualified his remark. "Oh, certainly you know your quantum physics and subspace theory. You're studied in scientific concepts that make the average techno-drone worker a lower primate in comparison to you, if knowledge is the standard. But you have always, sadly, lacked sophistication about anything else. Science in the empire is more than knowing how the universe works. All that is meaningless if you don't know how politics works. How people work. And how you can put them to work for you."

T'sart tapped a few more codes into the controls, then retrieved his weapon. "Much like I've put you to work for me." He walked around her, keeping the disruptor trained on her midsection nonchalantly, as if she was a small threat, but only that.

He stepped onto the transporter dais. "You'll find the controls locked in a very special way. If you try to stop me as I'm dematerializing, you'll likely burn your fingers from the forced overload and then a second later find yourself electrocuted." He holstered the weapon and leaned down, his eyes gleaming. "That's the theme today, isn't it? Forced overload."

The hum began low, then rose in pitch as light sparkled around him . . . and he was gone.

She'd done nothing to stop him.

Folan vaulted from the turbolift and to the bridge's science station. A few finger flicks on the console and she was running rapidly through her experiment-monitoring programs. Data scrolled past her view. She absorbed large chunks of it, but ignored those things that didn't interest her. She was looking for something specific and telltale. Something of T'sart's.

It scrolled past, and she had to roll the screens back. She pounded at the controls until the line of code came into view. When it did, and she could study the commands with his code signature, she could quickly follow the pattern to their logical conclusions.

He wouldn't have beamed to a planet. He would have beamed to a ship. A waiting ship.

"Medric, I want sensors repaired now. Before his ship's ion trail is gone!"

From his engineering station, Medric turned. "Whose?"

"T'sart! He's sabotaged my experiment, destroyed the other ships, wrecked havoc on the planet below. He must be stopped!"

What she was saying seemed insane, even to herself. How could she know what had happened outside the ship? And wasn't she merely blaming someone else for her grave errors?

And then it hit her—why would he leave her alive? Why would he destroy all those ships but hers?

Of course—he needed to escape. But now he'd done that. He'd have no more use for the *Makluan* now.

His theme, she thought. "Medric, check the engines. Are they on a buildup to overload?"

He shook his head. "I would be alerted—"

"Ignore your panel. It may have been tampered with. Scan the ship with a tricorder! Do it now!"

Medric opened the storage compartment and took

out a tricorder. He scanned, moving it around him. Unnecessarily, Folan thought. She waited for his answer, her tight chest barely letting her breathe.

He looked up suddenly, surprised. "We have less than five minutes before the core implodes."

"Get down there," Folan ordered. "Now!"

Medric collapsed into the chair at his bridge station. When he and Engineering finally were able to reverse the engine overload, thirty-three seconds remained before implosion.

Everyone felt relieved save Folan. She looked back to her library computer. It was all T'sart. He'd made it look like it was her own experiment, but it was him.

She knew there was nothing to be done except find him, catch him, and make him pay. "We need to get underway."

Medric looked at her incredulously. "Folan," he said, "you may have rank for technical command, but we have a crippled ship and our first duty is to that, and to our commander on the planet. We will find Commander J'emery and—"

"Commander J'emery is dead," Folan growled, frustrated. Didn't he understand? Didn't he see how many T'sart had killed? "He's murdered anyone who could stop him. He's insane."

Or you are. Of course no one said that, but it was etched into every expression. Especially Medric's.

It didn't matter. She was in charge. She was in command.

"Do as I say, Medric. We must get underway! *Now!*"

Silence dominated and Medric held still.

The other bridge officers waited. Waited to see who would do what, and which side would triumph so that they might choose the winner.

Finally, Medric spoke. "No."

Chapter Eleven

U.S.S. Enterprise, NCC-1701-E
Romulan Space
Sector 94

"TWENTY-TWO MINUTES NOW, SIR." Will Riker sighed, shook his head, and tried to dissipate a lead-dense tension. "If it's a trap, they're late for it."

"Or we're early," Picard said wryly. "But I doubt both."

Enterprise had been waiting at the appointed rendezvous coordinates. And waiting, and waiting. Every moment in Romulan space was risking a confrontation. And if that led to war, it would be one that couldn't be easily won, thanks to a hard-fought victory against the Dominion and an almost complete lack of subspace communications.

Another eight minutes, the captain thought as he

leaned back in the command chair. Thirty minutes of leeway was all Starfleet's orders had called for, unless Picard thought something was to be gained by extending the time. Of course, he'd have to justify the extension to his superiors.

Another minute crawled by, and the captain wasn't sure he'd want to extend the time. He tried to keep his personal feelings out of the equation. He couldn't let *Enterprise* slip into Romulan hands for any reason, and he couldn't start an all-out war.

"Long-range scan," Picard ordered.

"Still picking up indications of subspace radiation from Section 72, sir." Data paused and checked his readout again. "No vessels within range of scanners."

That told Picard little. Subspace radiation could mean anything—a fleet of freighters, a fleet of starships, or any mass of vessels in between. "Try to pinpoint the source to a star system."

"Aye, sir." Data hovered over his sensors a bit, then ran his hands so quickly over the console that his fingers were almost a blur. "Could be the Ch'chiknas system, or the Merterbis system."

The captain leaned forward. "Information on both systems?"

Wavering for a moment as the screen changed, the forward viewer's starscape shifted to a data readout.

"Ch'chiknas is uninhabited except for a few mining colonies. Four planets, a large asteroid belt. Merterbis has a thriving colony with both civilian and military population. Seven planets, one Class M."

"Distance from Merterbis?"

"Seven point three parsecs."

"Okay," Riker said. "We know where, but we don't know what."

Picard pulled in a deep breath. The comment reminded him of the problems with the dead zones. He knew where they were happening, but not *what* they were. And that's what he wanted to be thinking about more than all the Romulan machinations. Then again . . . Spock . . . he wanted to solve that, too.

"Keep up the passive scans," he ordered finally. "I'd like to know more, but we can't give our position away with an active beam."

Data nodded, and as the main viewer's picture returned to the starscape outside, Picard wondered just how much longer he would wait once the thirty-minute limit passed.

Romulan Warbird *Makluan*
In Orbit, Merterbis Colony
Romulan Space

"No." A simple word. A small word in most languages. It is often the first word learned by children, and the first forgotten by them as well. Medric's mutiny snapped like lightning and ricocheted across the bridge.

In the silence that followed the moment, Folan searched her subordinate's eyes. Was he truly going to challenge his superior and take her command? Or was it simply a test? From the set of his jaw and the angle in his brow, she knew it was both.

She wanted to glance around the bridge, meet the eyes of the others under her new command. She would be able to gain strength from their expressions if they were as outraged as she. But she would lose her own strength if she looked and their expressions were as frightened as her own.

Without moving her eyes from Medric's gaze, Folan roughly thumbed a button on the console next to her. "Security, stand by."

"Security here. Standing by, Sub-Commander."

Folan nodded, but still her glare was unmoved. "You have choices, I have choices."

Stone-faced but certainly sweating under his uniform, Medric lost when he began to argue. "You are not command—"

"I am *in* command. And I will stay in command until the Empire sees fit to replace me. But *you* are not the Empire, Medric. You are not the Praetor, and you are not the commander. You are Centurion Medric, engineering officer, and you are quickly on your way to being less than that."

From the corner of her eye, Folan was sure she saw a few bridge officers nod. Medric's mistake was in trying to discuss his point. As Folan was only now learning, respect in the Empire was not gained through debate and reason, but by strength, and courage.

"How soon can sensors and propulsion be repaired enough to get underway?"

"Twenty minutes," Medric answered.

She nodded. "See to it."

Finally, after a long moment, he turned to act on his

orders. But Medric was not weak. Yes, he'd shown the weakness of his position, but as he turned away in acceptance of it, Folan sensed he, too, had learned something today.

Not, Folan thought, *a relaxing thought.*

U.S.S. Enterprise, NCC 1701-E
Romulan Space
Sector 94

"Captain, we're picking up a vessel. One fifteen mark twelve."

Tensing, Picard leaned forward in the command chair. "Engage active scan." Switching from passive would make the *Enterprise* more noticeable to any Romulan sensor nets, but they'd be able to get a high degree of detail from the approaching ship.

"Switching," Data said. "Romulan shuttle, sir. Warp capable. Private craft, not military. Two life forms . . . both Romulan."

"Who?" Picard asked himself. "And who else?"

Riker shrugged. "Could be a decoy."

That thought had surely occurred to everyone, especially Picard. And as the sharply angled craft grew on the main viewer, the captain wondered just what sorts of traps the Romulans might lay, if this were all indeed some ruse.

Was the shuttle a giant explosive device that would gain proximity to *Enterprise* and disable the ship for the waiting cloaked birds-of-prey? Were the two Romulans on board contaminated with a bio-weapon that would render the *Enterprise* crew helpless and open to capture? He had to be open to all possibilities. At least all those he could conceive.

Bottom line though, while Picard could formulate a hundred different contingencies, none of them were helpful until a real, concrete problem actually presented itself.

"Open up a narrow-beam channel to the shuttle, Mr. Data." Picard rose, straightened his tunic. "Starfleet frequency, Code Alpha-Two."

Data turned back toward his captain a moment. "Starfleet Code A-2, sir?"

"Code Alpha-Two, Mr. Data."

The android turned back, his brow raised in a slight arc of surprise. "Aye, sir. Channel open."

"Send to shuttle: 'This is the Federation Starship *Enterprise*. Return identity response required.' "

"Hmm. Response in Code Alpha-Two, sir," Data said. "They are requesting approach for docking."

The captain pursed his lips and he felt his muscles tense. It was a test, but not much of one. Starfleet Code Alpha-Two was an encryption the Romulans hadn't broken, but one Spock would know. Of course, it had been determined that whoever was orchestrating the defection had access to Spock's codes. The only thing Picard had really learned was that Spock didn't have those codes to himself anymore. The Romulans on board the shuttle had them. That might very well mean that Spock was dead.

That thought chilled Picard's spine. "Security

detail report to shuttlebay. Mr. Data, send to shuttle—"

Data cut him off. "Captain, the shuttle has just raised
shields."

Picard hesitated only a millisecond. "Yellow alert."

From tactical, Lieutenant Chamberlain started ma-
nipulating the console's controls. "Aye, sir. Energizing
defense fields."

"Data, full-power scanning. Weapons on that shuttle?"

"Nothing detectable at this distance, sir. But I am now
reading one Romulan warbird at extreme sensor range."

The captain stalked forward and glared over Data's
shoulder. "That's why the shields. They're reacting to
the warbird being chased."

"Warbird is aware of us, Captain," Chamberlain
called. "We're being scanned."

"Counter-measures, Lieutenant. Jam their sensors as
best you can. If they must know there's another ship
here, let them guess what kind."

"The shuttle is increasing speed, sir." Data tapped at
his console and turned his head slightly up toward the
captain. "ETA is now four minutes."

Picard pivoted back toward the upper bridge. "Details on the warbird?"

"Sketchy." Riker, leaning over Chamberlain at the
tactical board, shook his head. "But we're reading
plasma leaks, and they're obviously not coming in
cloaked. They're firing disruptors at the shuttle."

"Damage to the shuttle?"

"Shields are weakening."

This all felt wrong to Picard. It all seemed too fast

and too much like an incident designed to get the *Enterprise* into battle in Romulan space. And yet . . .

"Set an intercept course for the shuttle." Picard dropped himself into the command chair. "Raise shields. Red alert."

"Course laid in, sir."

"Engage."

Enterprise sped forward, and in little more than an instant the Romulan shuttle grew from a small dot into a fist-sized bubble on the main viewscreen.

"Captain, the warbird is continuing to fire on the Romulan shuttle," Data reported.

"I'd warn them off if I thought that would accomplish anything."

"Might anger them," Riker offered.

"They seem quite upset now, sir," Data said. "The shuttle's shields are collapsing."

"Extend our shields around them, sir?" Riker asked.

That was a risky undertaking, and there were too many unanswered questions. Not only would extending the shields around another vessel put a high drain on the ship's power, it would leave the *Enterprise* vulnerable. If the shuttle *were* a decoy . . .

"Transporter range?"

"We'll have to drop shields." Riker's voice showed no strain.

Dropping shields completely might be more risky. Were the shuttle a decoy, when shields are down both it and the warbird could attack and the *Enterprise* would be defenseless. Picard hated decisions that amounted to choosing between the lesser of two evils. Still, he had to choose. "We won't have to drop shields if we take your suggestion and extend ours around them. Make it so."

"And lock weapons on the warbird?" Riker asked.

"Yes. But hold fire." The captain leaned toward a status monitor at his side. "Data, lock transporters on the two life-forms in the shuttle. Beam them, on my mark, directly to the bridge as soon as our shields are around their vessel. Hold any possible weapons they're carrying in the pattern buffers."

"Aye, sir. Transporter locked."

Picard pressed a button on the arm of his chair. "Security detail, to the bridge."

"Warbird is within weapons range," Chamberlain reported.

"Shuttle has lost shields."

"Now, Data! Extend our shields and energize."

"Romulans are firing!" said Chamberlain.

Light played out across the viewscreen as the warbird's disruptors punched into the shuttle. *Enterprise*'s shields protected the small vessel, but both ships were buffeted by the impact.

"Tractor that into the shuttlebay," Picard ordered, indicating the small Romulan vessel.

Four security guards poured out the turbolifts as the glare of two transporter columns filled the lower bridge with sparkle.

The guards stood ready, and as the two Romulan figures solidified, Picard nodded the security men closer.

"Warbird turning on us," Riker called.

"Evasive," Picard said, and took a moment to glance toward the two Romulans.

"Captain Picard." The Romulan on the left stepped forward and nodded. "As usual, the *Enterprise*'s timing was impeccable."

Picard stepped forward, his mouth open just the slightest in surprise. He nearly gasped, but instead his lips curled into a thin smile. "Spock."

Chapter Twelve

**U.S.S. Enterprise, NCC 1701-E
Romulan Space
Sector 94**

"EVASIVE," PICARD ORDERED, his respectful gaze lingering on Spock a moment. The warbird fired weak shots across the *Enterprise*'s shields, but at point-blank it was enough to rattle the ship.

"We are being hailed, sir," Shapiro said.

"My apologies, Captain," the Romulan with Spock said. "I did think that my arrangements would have been sufficient that we wouldn't be pursued."

"*Your* arrangements?" The captain stared at the Romulan a moment, but he didn't have time to figure it all out now.

"On screen."

"Picard. When I saw it was your ship, I didn't want to believe it."

"Folan—" She was seething with hate, he could tell. Her eyes got small and she leaned forward in her command chair.

"Surrender, and prepare to be boarded—or be destroyed." She turned away in her chair, and the screen went blank.

"Get us out of here," Picard ordered.

Turning on his heel as the *Enterprise* also turned away, he nodded at the two security guards by the forward turbolift to stand ready, but at ease.

Smoothly, the guards marched toward Spock and the Romulan, stopping a few feet away, as Picard lowered himself into the command chair. "Avoid offensive fire, Mr. Chamberlain. Helm, plot a direct course out of Romulan space." The captain looked up at Spock and his companion. After a long moment, it dawned on Picard just who the Romulan was. He rose, slowly. "T'sart," he whispered.

T'sart smiled and bowed his head as if accepting a compliment.

Blood seemed to rush to Picard's fingertips and face. He felt warm. He felt angry. Finally, he ground out: "Under the authority of the Supreme Court of the United Federation of Planets, and the Attorney General of the Federation Council, you are hereby placed under Federation arrest. You have the right to refuse interrogation, and the right to legal representation."

T'sart's angled features fell into a deep frown. "Ah,

but Captain, I'm here to ask the Federation for political asylum."

Disruptor shots sizzled against the shields, and as the bridge shook around them, only the security guards and Spock seemed unaffected.

"Direct course plotted and on the screen, sir."

"Engage." Picard spun toward tactical. "Lieutenant, disable their weapons and propulsion." He tapped at his comm badge. "Dr. Crusher, report to the bridge."

Another glance of weapons fire against the shields rattled the ship. Less so as *Enterprise* accelerated away from the damaged warbird.

The captain stood again, and took just a few steps toward T'sart, Spock, and the guards. "You have a lot of gall, T'sart." He nodded to the guards. "The brig."

The security men nodded, and motioned T'sart toward the turbolift.

"Captain, you're making a mistake," T'sart said. "Destroy Folan now—while you have the chance."

Picard remained silent, his orders unchanging.

"Tell him, Spock. Tell him *you* understand the stakes."

"Get him out of here," Picard told the guards.

Smiling a hateful, condescending smile, T'sart went with them. "We'll talk soon, Captain. Very soon. And then you'll regret your actions here." The lift door closed and the last words echoed away.

"Warbird weapons are disabled, Captain. They're following, but falling behind. Recommend breaking off attempt to disable their engines. They can't catch up at their present speed, and they know where we're going anyway."

"Very good. Make it so, Number One."

The turbolift doors parted and Dr. Beverly Crusher stepped out.

"Captain." Beverly greeted him a bit distractedly as she stepped to the lower bridge. She nodded to Spock. "Ambassador. The captain didn't tell me we were expecting you for certain."

"Nothing *was* certain," Spock said, returning her greeting, then looking toward Picard. "Captain, we must talk."

Picard nodded. "Indeed. Doctor, please join us. Number One, you have the bridge."

The captain marched toward his ready room, Spock and Beverly in tow.

Spock wasn't indignant, of course. He didn't even ask about the procedure. He would have ordered the same in Picard's place.

Beverly ran her tricorder scanner over Spock a second time. "DNA match is flawless. No sign of any known gene-masking elements. But his vitals are still showing up as Romulan, not Vulcan."

"My apologies, Doctor," Spock said and closed his eyes for a moment.

Picard looked from Spock to Beverly. The doctor's brows rose a moment, then she smiled slightly, thin red lips curling up. "And now back to Vulcan. That's amazing. No sign of any metabolic drugs."

"The Romulan transport centers have sensor screens that would alert operators to both vital sign anomalies and altering drugs. They do not, however, scan for differences between Romulan and Vulcan DNA."

"The difference would be minute. I assume there are even some Romulans who could pass for Vulcan on most DNA scans." Beverly stored her small hand sensor in her medical tricorder and put both in a holster at her side under her tunic jacket.

"Five point three-nine-one percent of the Romulan population, to be exact," Spock offered.

"Thank you, Doctor," Picard said. "Now check our prisoner in the brig. Dismissed."

Somberly, the doctor nodded, and left the room.

When they were alone, Picard said, "Did T'sart find you, discover your presence, and you didn't feel you could kill him?" He maneuvered to sit at his desk, and motioned Spock to take a chair in front of him. They both sat.

"Not exactly," Spock said.

Being in Spock's presence had an almost ceremonial feeling to it. Picard knew Spock well enough to have had a Vulcan mind-meld bond with him at one time, and yet . . . talking to him was as odd and humbling as speaking with a page out of history. Picard muted a chuckle. He'd done that, with Kirk, with Zefram Cochrane, with K'mpec, with Montgomery Scott, and a few others . . . but he'd never get used to it.

After a few moments of these thoughts, Picard finally spoke. "I can't imagine you'd allow yourself to be coerced into helping T'sart. But if you captured him—"

"I did not. I suppose, if anything, you might call it a mutual capture."

"Explain." For the slightest of moments Picard wondered if his tone was too demanding. But he was a captain, and it was his natural tone. Spock had been a starship captain himself. He understood.

Spock tipped his head to one side. "I could not continue toward my goal on Romulus under the risk that T'sart would expose me. He could not attain his goal without my assistance. Who was controlling whom is a semantic question. We each needed the other."

"How did he learn of your existence?" Picard asked. "And how do you know he told no one else?"

"I cannot answer either question with comfortable certainty. T'sart has a network of operatives, some of whom work for him out of loyalty, some of whom work from fear, and some unknowingly or unwittingly. I believe few, if any, know what his goals are at any one time. I trust him when he tells me he is the only government official to know of my presence, but only because it was within his best interests for me to remain hidden from their attentions."

"And that goal is?"

Spock's body took on the slightest of tensions. "Seemingly benign. Which I do not believe in full. But there is no doubting his data and the proof he's offered me. Which is why I needed to make contact and return to the Federation for now. The galaxy is in extreme danger . . . and T'sart knows why."

"The dead zones," Picard said. He felt his own muscles tense.

Spock nodded. "Indeed."

"Not only in Federation space, but . . ."

"If T'sart's data is correct, and I believe it to be, throughout the galaxy as well."

U.S.S. Voyager, NCC-74656
Unexplored sector
Delta Quadrant

"Tactical." Captain Kathryn Janeway absorbed the display in an instant and then pivoted toward her command chair. "Warp, evasive! Tom, get us out of here. Or at least keep us out of their weapons range."

"Trying, Captain." Tom Paris pounded at the navigation console and *Voyager*'s engines whined as she accelerated into warp. The Borg cube pursued.

"Mr. Kim, any particular explanation as to how the Borg managed to sneak up on us?" Janeway asked.

Ensign Harry Kim shook his dark head. "No, ma'am. Scanners are still fluctuating. Diagnostics show no malfunctions. I just can't seem to scan certain areas of space."

Why? Janeway wondered, but would have to ask herself that later.

"Get Seven up here. Maybe she has some insights."

Chakotay nodded and thumbed the intercom in the arm of his chair. "Seven of Nine, report to the bridge."

"Captain," Harry called, "they're hailing us, but the subspace frequency is breaking up."

Janeway shook her head. How could that be? "At this range?"

Double-checking his findings, Harry nodded once. "Yes, ma'am."

"Let's hear it."

The young ensign tapped at his console.

"*We are th . . . Borg. You will be assim . . . Your biolog . . . nilogical distinctiveness will be . . . to our own. Resistance is futile.*"

Seven strode from the turbolift and marched straight to Janeway. "Something is wrong. I am unable to sense the collective."

"That's a good thing, I'd think," Paris said.

"Good or not," Seven said, with some amount of fear in her tone, "I should be able to. I cannot."

"Then it's not our problem receiving them . . . it's their ability to send?" Chakotay asked.

"I do not know," Seven replied, and Janeway sensed that was what frightened the former drone the most.

"Captain, the cube is accelerating toward us," Tuvok reported.

"Tom, Z plus seven light days, warp nine on my mark."

Paris steadied himself and readied the ship at his fingertips.

Motioning for Seven to take a seat, Janeway lowered herself into her own chair. "Now!"

Voyager groaned as she twisted against physics, leaping up quickly as the Borg cube vessel hurtled past. Janeway heard Torres over the comm, complaining about a plasma leak or inertial dampers, or both.

"Forward course now, Mr. Paris. Warp two," Janeway called, and with that order the bridge crew, and *Voyager* herself, seemed to sigh.

"Tactical on the Borg?"

"They are . . ." Tuvok paused, and that alone made

Janeway twist toward him. Anything that would stagger the Vulcan's comments . . .

"They are," he continued, "dead in space."

The bridge fell silent, and all eyes turned toward Seven, including Janeway's.

Seven looked stunned. But then again, so did Harry, and had she not been a more experienced captain, perhaps so might have Janeway.

"Mr. Paris," Janeway said.

"Captain?"

"Take us within scanning range of the cube. I want to know what happened to it."

Paris pulled in a deep breath and let out a sigh. "Aye, Captain."

Janeway checked and rechecked Ensign Kim's station scanners for the third time. That wasn't making their situation better.

"Captain, holographic emitters don't seem to be working. The doctor has transferred himself to the mobile emitter. That's working for now."

Janeway nodded and walked over to Tuvok's station. "Thank you, Chakotay." She tapped an intercom button on the tactical station. "Janeway to Engineering."

"Torres here, Captain. Still can't get warp power online. Nothing's wrong with the equipment, we just can't generate a matter/antimatter subspace reaction. I'd say we were in the same boat as the Borg."

"I don't suppose this is more of that chaotic space we've come into contact with."

Seven shook her head once, firmly. "This is *not*

chaotic space. It has none of the characteristics that we, or the Borg, have encountered as such."

"I'm forced to agree, Captain," Tuvok said.

Janeway sighed. "Desperate hope. Before too long we're going to run out of battery power. Mr. Paris, use thrusters. Full reverse course."

"That'll be pretty slow going, Captain."

"I'm open to other options." Janeway turned, looking from Tuvok, to Harry Kim, to Chakotay, to Seven, then to Paris again. "Anyone?" In her mind's eye she thought of Torres as well, who also remained silent over the comm.

"Thrusters," Paris said. "Aye."

The captain chuckled tightly. "Tuvok," she prodded, shaking her head. "Tell me *something*."

"I have nothing more, Captain. Warp and impulse power circuits are intact, but energy is simply not there."

"Seven?"

"This is nothing I am familiar with, Captain. Obviously, even the Borg cube is trapped."

"We can't just sit here," Janeway said, stomping down to the command chair. "We have thirty hours of battery power. Thrusters won't last that long, and even that course is assuming there's some dampening field in this area of space. We could be wrong about that. In the meantime, I suggest we find out what else could be happening."

"*Yes, Captain.*" Torres said, and Seven said the same a second later.

Chakotay stood. "I'll give Seven a hand in astrometrics."

"Good." Janeway nodded up to him, then rose herself. "I'll go to engineering. Like I said: we can't just sit here."

"No, ma'am." Chakotay smiled and let her step toward the turbolift first. "Thirty hours. Should be enough time to find an answer."

"If . . ." Janeway whispered as the lift doors opened, "if there *is* an answer."

Chapter Thirteen

U.S.S. Enterprise, NCC 1701-E
Romulan Space
Sector 87

"AUXILIARY POWER. Reinforce those starboard shields. Status of the brig?" Picard grappled with the slice of inner bulkhead that had collapsed in his way. Just how the Romulan warbird had been able to catch up so quickly, he wasn't sure. But again, he wondered if all of this was some Romulan ruse.

"Damage to that deck and the two surrounding decks, sir. No hull breaches, but internal structural collapse in some areas."

The captain grunted as he moved a large ceiling plate from his path. "I can see that, Number One. Where is the warbird now?"

"They fell behind again, but we're leaking a trail of coolant that won't dissipate soon."

"Understood. Picard out." Suddenly the debris was much lighter in Picard's hands, and he turned to find Spock helping heft it out of the way. "Ambassador."

"Spock will suffice, Captain."

"I appreciate the help, Spock, but—"

"Neither of us should logically be here, Captain. Most certainly we should let damage control crews clear the debris between here and your brig. With your permission, I will not wait."

"Are you saying you're doing something illogical?"

"Impractical, perhaps."

"The practical isn't the logical?"

"Ofttimes not."

Picard couldn't help but smile as Spock lifted the last large part of the ceiling that had been blocking the corridor. Here was this man, this Starfleet legend, this Vulcan statesman, clearing rubbish from a collapsing ceiling, debating philosophy, and not even breaking a sweat.

"It might be practical," Spock continued as he and Picard stepped over the downed wire and insulation dust that littered the hallway, "to let those who are qualified clear the corridor. But I can think of nothing more logical than assuming T'sart is uninjured and working against his harried guards, and therefore we should attend at once."

The captain could not help but agree. T'sart was suddenly very important. If he, in fact, knew what the dead zones were and why . . . Picard's only problem was that

T'sart had shown Spock only limited proof. Enough proof that Spock believed the Romulan, but not enough to answer all questions. Picard wanted to see that data, and more. And if T'sart was dead, perhaps the data would be lost with him.

What an odd position Picard had found himself in . . . hoping a mass murderer was alive and well.

One last corner turned, and the brig expanded before them. Twelve large cells, each protected by transporter-resistant materials and battery-backed-up force-field doors. T'sart's was still intact, his guards unconscious under a collapsed support beam that had fallen. The beam now leaned onto the doorway, its end being held up by the sizzling electro-field that locked T'sart into his cell.

"A few more days and that would drain the field completely," Picard muttered.

"I should protest formally," T'sart said as the captain and Spock approached. "Surely you have better accommodations for guests than a collapsing brig."

"For guests, yes." Picard checked one of the panels outside the shielded archway that opened into T'sart's cell. He turned to Spock. "Radiation leaks. We have to evacuate this whole section."

Spock nodded and pulled the two guards free while Picard upholstered his phaser and aimed the weapon toward T'sart. "Stand back." He lowered the field door and the support beam clattered loudly to the deck.

"I'm no threat to you, Captain," T'sart said, smiling.

A smile on a face so Vulcan was jarring, Picard thought, and he glanced a moment at Spock. Had he ever smiled? Surely, when he was under his Romulan guise he must have. But, ever else?

"You're so much of a threat," Picard said finally, "that you've had to promise to quell a larger threat to assure yourself safe passage. Rest assured, I won't hesitate to stun you with little provocation."

T'sart stepped lightly over the debris on the floor and out of his cell. "Yes," he said dryly. "That is both a restful and assuring thought."

"What is your current heading, Captain?"

Silence followed T'sart's question. The *Enterprise* officers seated around the briefing table looked to Picard to see what his answer would be. He made none. He simply ignored the Romulan.

"Status, Number One?"

"He seems pretty demanding for a prisoner." Riker said.

"Ship's status."

Riker nodded to Chief Engineer Geordi La Forge, who tapped at the computer in front of him. A graphic of the damaged sections appeared on the viewscreen. "Minor structural damage. Brig area still has radiation leaks. We're working on cleaning it up, but it will take some time. We've secured some quarters for our . . . *guest* here, and made sure they're safe."

"Exhilarating, that my previously sworn enemies have my well-being so high among their priorities."

Chief Engineer Geordi La Forge swiveled around. "We've made it safe *from* you, not for you."

"This ship," Picard said, turning toward T'sart, "is in this condition only because we have you aboard. And you're only aboard because Ambassador Spock has verified that you, in fact, have data on the cause of these dead zones."

"Dead zones," T'sart said. "Interesting term for it. More accurate than you might think."

"I want to know what you've proven to Spock," Picard continued, "and more. You're to work with Lieutenant Commander Data—"

"Don't presume to give me orders, Picard." There was an anger in T'sart's voice that surprised Picard a bit. He was sure not to let that surprise show in his expression, but one could see just how much of a facade T'sart's pleasantries were.

"You're on my ship, T'sart," Picard said. "My orders, my rules. You're here for a reason. Several reasons, in fact, I'm sure. For now, we'll deal with the one you'll admit to."

T'sart smiled. "Captain, you wound me with such a belligerent attitude." He was obviously quick to regain his composure. "Should you continue to be so, you'll wound yourself . . . and every living thing in this galaxy."

Picard pulled in a deep breath and released it slowly, not quite sighing. "Ambassador?"

T'sart turned toward Spock, who sat at Picard's right. Past Spock were Data and Deanna Troi. Both also turned and listened intently as the Vulcan began to speak.

"What the Federation is calling 'dead zones,' the Romulans have dubbed 'power deserts.' Increasingly, there are many names for this new phenomenon. Reports from all over the Alpha Quadrant demonstrate just how widespread this problem is. Three Romulan colonies have needed to be evacuated on a massive scale. Captain Picard has informed me that seven much smaller Federation colonies have suffered the same need. Reports from almost every sector in the Federation confirmed that these zones, where higher energy technology has null output, have spread. Contact has been lost with Starbase 244, Starbase 15, and Deep Space Nine, just to name a few. All have gone silent; it is assumed all are victims of this phenomenon."

"And you know what's causing this?" Riker asked T'sart.

The Romulan was silent for a moment, and Picard wondered if he was merely lost in thought, or was choosing his words so that whatever he said would benefit him the most. "Is it actually my turn to comment? I was wondering when you'd finally ask the one person who knows more than anyone on this topic."

"Just tell us what you know," Picard ordered.

T'sart's brows drew up, and then his face took on a harshness that surprised even the captain. "You want to hear it all, Captain?" The rank was voiced as an insult. "Brace yourself, and when I'm finished, act quickly, or we're all soon dead."

The room was uncomfortable, silent, as T'sart focused all attention on himself.

"I know from where the phenomenon emanates. I

know how we can get there, and I know what we must do to stop it."

"Can we only stop it? What about reversing it? Can't we make these 'dead zones' come back to life?" Deanna asked.

T'sart smiled his condescending smile. "Young child, how easy is it to come back from the dead?"

"Difficult," Spock said. "But not impossible."

An odd silence followed, all eyes on Spock, as if he had more to say. He did not. He merely raised a brow at Picard.

"Where is the proof of what you say? Why didn't you bring it with you?" Picard asked.

"Some things are not even possible for me, Picard. Secreting a Romulan warbird's memory banks in my pocket . . . someone would have asked why I was on board and why I was using the computer so extensively. I showed Spock some of the data from a Romulan computer console. Had we lingered long enough even to copy much of what we viewed, we would both be dead now. You wouldn't have wanted that, would you?"

Picard hated this man's smile. It was a smile that had radiated over how many deaths? A million? More? To see it here and not be able to wipe it off this murderer's face . . .

And he *was* a murderer, wanted by any number of governments, including the Federation. Every Starfleet captain had standing orders to arrest T'sart should they find him within their grasp. Well, here T'sart was. Picard should just return to Starbase 10 with Spock and turn T'sart over to starbase security. That was what the regulations would tell him.

Normally he would contact Starfleet, explain the situation, make his own suggestions, and await orders. Nothing was normal now. There was no Starfleet Command. At least not unless the *Enterprise* traveled to it herself.

This decision was his, and his alone. How he could trust someone like T'sart was the real question. And the answer was, he couldn't. But he could trust Spock. Spock had seen some preliminary data that had convinced him.

"Spock, can you use the *Enterprise* computers to recreate the information you saw?"

"It should be possible to relate what I saw, but those were conclusions, and brief scraps of supporting data. Not enough to initiate our own research."

"It's more than we have now. Please work with Commander Data."

Spock nodded.

"No need," T'sart said, and pulled a thin Romulan data crystal from his tunic pocket.

"I thought you said you had no data."

"I said I couldn't get *all* of it. I did manage to save my personal files."

Frowning, the captain tapped a button on a small computer console in the table. "Computer, please give computer access to Spock, former Vulcan Ambassador, retired. Starfleet officer, retired."

"Acknowledged. Access confirmed: Spock. Rank: Captain. Temporary Starfleet activation necessary."

A slight chuckle rose in the back of Picard's throat.

"Welcome back to Starfleet, Captain Spock. At least temporarily."

Spock nodded his acceptance, but said nothing else.

"Well," T'sart said, his lips pressed into a thin line. "If you're finished with your pomp and flourish . . . You're sitting here as if I haven't just told you life is ending as you know it. It is. Life in all ways may be ending. Do you understand this?"

"I understand," Picard said. "We have a problem of galactic—"

"The galaxy?" T'sart scoffed. "Nothing so mundane. I suspect this problem will soon be universal."

"As in the *entire* universe?" Riker said, dubious.

T'sart looked at him. "How many people did you have to bribe to attain such a high rank?"

"That's enough," Picard barked.

"Oh, I think not," T'sart snapped back. "You fail to grasp the gravity of this situation. We don't even have time for the lecture I seem to have to give. Do you understand what these dead zones mean? We're not just talking about the end of subspace communications, the lack of which has already destabilized the most powerful governments in this quadrant. We're not just going to see the end of interstellar exploration. We're on the verge of every space-faring civilization collapsing completely. How many of your colonies will grow cold without their power plants? How many will starve on your Terran homeworld when the replicators don't work? How many will die in your hospitals because it is high technology that cures your disease and deformity?"

Factories, transportation, communication, air purification and creation, heat . . . and light. All technology at risk. Picard's mind boggled at the idea.

"The lucky ones will die quickly, Captain, of suffocation or hypothermia. The unlucky ones, on your homeworld and mine, will fall into the barbarism and warfare that comes when billions must share the tiny resources that can sustain only a few. And it will happen soon, Picard. Not in months or weeks, but in days, or even hours."

Picard glanced quickly at Spock. The Vulcan gave a slight, grave, affirming nod. His message was clear—what T'sart was saying was chillingly accurate.

"I understand, T'sart," Picard said.

"I hope you do," the Romulan said. "Because it won't just be the Federation or the Empire that will suffer. We're not the only power-addicted civilizations. Everyone, everywhere, who has a technology greater than post-industrialization will fall and then stagnate. Trillions upon trillions of lives will be lost, because the number of people a warp-faring race can sustain is too great for any lesser science."

"And your solution is?"

"Stop it, at the source." T'sart said. "The Caltiskan system."

Picard swiveled his chair toward Spock.

The Vulcan thought for only a semi-second. "That's most of the way across Romulan space, Captain."

Picard nodded. "Near the Klingon/Romulan border." He shook his head. "You want us to take the *Enterprise* right through the center of the Romulan Empire, coming within ten parsecs of the Romulan homeworld?"

"No, *you* want to. You don't want to waste time, either. Because the longer you wait, the greater the chance we won't be able to get there at all. And if we don't, Picard . . ." T'sart motioned with his hand, including the entire ship in one slow, sweeping gesture. "All this will be nothing more than floating debris, cold and dead in space. There will be no more starships, and perhaps with enough time, no more stars."

"Even if I believe you," Picard said, "we can't just traverse the most densely populated part of the Romulan Empire."

"You can. With my help." T'sart picked up a data padd, tapped into it for a few moments and then slid the padd down the table toward Picard. "The subspace frequency of our cloaked ships. With this, you will know where every cloaked vessel in range of your scanners is located. You'll be able to destroy them, before they destroy you. And that's just what you'll have to do. And when you get to the Caltiskan system, you're going to have to surprise and overpower, or out-think, the Tal Shiar forces that even the proper Romulan government is unaware are there."

Picard snapped up the padd and glanced at the code. "You'd do this to your own people? Give us the power to see through their cloaks? Ask us to destroy them?"

T'sart smiled again. "The resonance frequency is changed every three days. If we accomplish our goal, there will actually be a fourth day and we can celebrate. If we don't, and either die trying or simply die in a dead zone . . . it will mean little to any of us." He nodded at the padd. "This code was changed yesterday. You have two days, Captain. Two days, and you'll be blind again. Sooner, if they learn we have the code, so we must use it wisely."

"We?"

"Of course, Captain. You can't have this party without me. I've told you where to go, not what to do when you get there. Puts a little more importance on my health than you otherwise might, don't you think?

"Oh, your health is paramount in my thoughts," Picard said, tapping his comm badge. "Helm, plot a course for Klingon space. Radio ahead, let them know we're coming."

"Aye, sir."

For the first time, T'sart's expression was one touched with what looked like just a bit of fear. It could have been anger, but Picard preferred to see it as panic. "Klingon space? You know the price on my head there. Those barbaric fools would destroy a planet to have me in their grasp. Why do you think I've given you the cloak code? You *must* go through Romulan space."

"Right now, I'd say the price on your head is about the same in Romulan space as it is in Klingon space," Picard said, allowing himself the slightest smile at T'sart's expense. "But the *Enterprise* can travel freely among the Klingons. And so long as they don't know we have you, you're safe."

T'sart pursed his lips again. "Fine, Picard. Gamble with my life. But by doing so, you gamble with your own, and that of the galaxy's. We don't have time for delays."

"I'll take that risk, T'sart. I told you," Picard handed the padd to Riker, *"I* am in command."

Romulan Warbird *Makluan*
Romulan Space
Sector 89

"I am in command," Folan said. "And I want priority on warp drive and cloaking systems."

"We should try to alert the fleet," Medric said. "We cannot do this alone."

"We're the only ones who *can* do this," Folan cried. "We still have them in scanner range. They'll be in the Neutral Zone soon and, once in Federation space, out of our grasp entirely."

Medric sighed. Folan sensed he was trying to obey her, but he thought so differently, and respected her so little. That wasn't her fault, however. But it was her burden to bear. Every moment she felt she needed to do something to bolster her standing in command. Is this how it is for J'emery, and all commanders, or only those who had been scientists?

"Sub-Commander," a centurion called. *"Enterprise* is changing course."

Folan pivoted toward the crewman and leaped up toward his station. "Away from the Neutral Zone?"

"No, Sub-Commander, but away from Federation space. They are on a course that will take them into Klingon space."

"Klingon space?" Folan's eyes narrowed in perplexity, then she turned to Medric, determined. "I need warp capability repaired now. We must be able to match their speed. Then I need the cloak, and communications as well."

Medric smiled. "You will call the fleet?"

Folan nodded slowly. "I will call for help," she said, almost in a whisper. "And T'sart . . . and Picard, will die."

Chapter Fourteen

U.S.S. Enterprise, NCC 1701-E
Romulan Space Sector 72
Shuttle Bay

AWAKENING SEQUENCE COMPLETE at timecode 4547.

Systems check: Internal scanners, nominal. External scanners, nominal. Active and passive sensor grids, nominal. Tractor systems, energized. Force-field generators, energized. Ordnance sub-systems, activated.

Verify directive: Undermine and inhibit subject's infrastructure.

Verify sub-directives: Avoid contact with biological forms. Avoid contact with sensor detection. Avoid disabling environments and events.

Scan for location . . . Interior of shuttle.

Plotting course for exploration outside shuttle. Plotted. Antigravity propulsion initiated and engaged on heading toward shuttle's port bulkhead.

Scanning obstacle bulkhead: plastiform constructs, various metallic alloys, circuitry. Point of weakness determined. Calculating . . . initiating disruptor burst. Vaporization complete.

Evacuation complete at timecode 4549.

Scanning shuttlebay . . . point of weakness determined . . .

Verify position . . . acquiring . . . Deck 12, section 9, subsection 2, internal Jefferies tube 5. Within range of conduit 31A.

Error: subject shielding interferes with attempt to reprogram.

Formulating solution . . .

Determination: physical manipulation necessary. Charging tractor nodes and force-field generators.

Charge complete. Initiating manipulation.

Alert triggered, bioform approaching. Disengage. Shutting down systems. Maneuvering against bulkhead for silent mode.

Postponing action until bioform exceeds scanner range . . .

Sleep state established.

Self-waking initiated. All bioforms outside of set range.

Resume previous directive . . .

Chapter Fifteen

U.S.S. Enterprise, NCC 1701-E
Klingon/Romulan border
Sector 23

Three days ago

"WHAT IS IT, SPOCK?"

Picard leaned over the Vulcan's shoulder and looked intently at the science station computer monitor.

"Something Mr. Data and I have found of interest." Spock swiveled his chair away from the console, and Picard stepped back as Data did the same. "In the small amount of information that T'sart was able to smuggle from his research, and by remembering what I was allowed to see of T'sart's 'proof,' there is perhaps evidence that these dead zone occurrences are but one stage in a continuous phenomenon. I had glanced at a table of statistics on the current Romulan dead zones. More recent appearances of these zones have allowed tractor beams and even disruptor weapons to function. As these zones . . . *age*, for lack of a better term, even those lower-level power usages become inactive."

"Lower level?" Picard asked.

"In comparison to the warp and impulse power generations, sir," Data replied.

The captain nodded. "How . . . far might this degenerate? Will chemical thrusters become useless? Atomic reactions? Need we replicate candles, Mr. Spock, in case we happen upon an older dead zone?"

Spock shook his head. "There is no way, given our limited data, to answer those questions. We will need to study an older zone, perhaps testing it from within."

"Let's hope we don't get *that* chance. I don't intend to replicate those candles."

"They'd do you little good, Captain," Spock said. "Unless you intended to replicate matches as well."

Picard smiled, and noticed a slight twinkle in the Vulcan's eye. "See what we can do about reconfiguring a probe that will work in these older zones, should we come close to one. If we can learn how to scan for them, map them . . ."

"Aye, sir," Data said.

Spock nodded and Picard stepped down toward the lower bridge.

Once both Data and Spock had turned back toward

the science station, the android leaned toward Spock and spoke in a slightly hushed tone.

"You suggested the captain replicate matches," Data said.

"Yes."

"That was a joke, was it not?"

Spock paused in his work a moment, turning to look at Data. "Without anything to light the candles, of what use would they be?"

"Hmm." Data considered that. "Indeed. I suppose it was not a joke. Or at least not a funny one. I can often tell now. Remember, since we first met, I have gained emotions."

Spock turned back to the console. "I remember. I hope not on my account."

"No, sir." Data also turned back to the console, but then a slight smile pulled his lips up and he glanced back. "*That* was a joke, was it not, sir?"

One brow raised in amusement, Spock was silent.

Romulan Warbird *Makluan*
Romulan/Klingon border
Sector 53

"Did the message get through?" Folan thought her vocal intensity sounded perhaps too nervous, despite her attempt at a demanding tone.

Medric turned tiredly from his console. "We have no way to know. Normally such a high-speed warp buoy would be destroyed entering enemy space. We should not have used our last one on such a task, in any case."

"I disagree. If this was our last chance for long-range communication, they are closer than our own forces." Folan stepped down to the command chair. *Her* command chair now. "Perhaps we could modify a warp probe?" So much to think about, so many possibilities. Command was new to her. And she had enemies to her command: T'sart, and Picard. And Medric.

"Subspace communication focusing coils can't be replicated, and we have no such inventory in storage," the centurion said, his tone suggesting she should have known that. "That, along with subspace travel being erratic at best the last two weeks . . ."

"Well, it was a calculated risk," Folan explained. That was another mistake, and she knew it the moment she'd heard it clatter to the floor. Medric had suddenly followed her down to the command deck.

"Had we used the buoy to send a message to the fleet—" he began.

She tried to shut him down quickly. "We would not have accomplished our ends." Folan turned away toward the main viewscreen.

"Your ends," Medric said, turning her chair harshly back toward him.

Folan was stunned for a moment, then reminded herself she needed to play the military game of authoritarian bravado and bluster. She tried to narrow her eyes and stare him down. "This is my command now, Medric. My ends *are* your ends, *our* ends."

As he always was when she showed her backbone,

Medric was silent. But his courage returned more quickly each time he confronted Folan, and this time he paused but a moment. "There is a difference between being in command, and commanding respect. We have seventy-four comrades dead, and twice that injured. We have no communications with Command. One disruptor bank is off-line and will take seven more hours to repair. We are leaking plasma from our starboard nacelle, rendering our cloak useless. We're limping. Just what is it you believe you command?"

Folan leaned toward him and whispered. "Be careful, Medric. A sharp tongue can swing so fast it slits its master's throat."

He considered that a moment, then stood straight, almost—but not quite—at attention. "At this time, I'm only making . . . a recommendation. There is an imperial subspace relay station just fourteen hours from here at present speed. Once within its range, perhaps it will boost our signal enough to notify Command and await orders. We might even be able to borrow a replacement—"

She shook her head. "We haven't the time. T'sart is almost in Klingon space. And reports before we left were that the subspace radio relays were having the same problems as all vessels and bases. No . . . we will assume our message was received and that our new allies will act properly."

"A large and foolish assumption," Medric said as he turned away. "Sub-Commander," he added finally.

"Mine to make." Folan pivoted back toward the main viewer again.

"For now," Medric whispered, probably only loud

enough for her to hear, but it was a scream into her mind. *For now.*

U.S.S. Enterprise, NCC 1701-E
Klingon/Romulan border
Sector 10

Picard and Riker walked briskly toward the turbolift, and more importantly, away from T'sart's quarters. That the Romulan was in quarters rather than the brig nagged at Picard, chafing his sensibilities.

"Someone with his personal death count, dictating to us," the captain grumbled.

"He's used to everyone jumping through his hoops," Riker said.

"Or he kills them and pushes them through." The captain shook his head. "Well, this ship is *not* at his service. And we know that few of our goals will be the same. He wants to use us, and we need to use him."

"Assuming he's not been lying from the start. He could have shown Spock false data. Could be feeding us the same." They passed a few crewmembers going the other direction, and Riker lowered his voice. "Perhaps the dead zones are T'sart's own invention. Mass murderers aren't known for their trustworthiness."

"And trust is the problem," Picard said. "Which puts us in an interesting position. We're looking to traverse Romulan space without permission, to attack a Romulan outpost. We are, essentially, taking the necessary steps to start another interstellar war."

"We do have Spock's belief that what T'sart said is true."

"Which is a great deal." Picard and Riker slipped into a turbolift. "Bridge," the captain ordered, then turned back to Riker. "I hope it's enough. Obviously we're not at all assuming our ignoble guest doesn't have some . . . trick up his sleeve, as it were."

"So many tricks up there I'd be surprised if he has room for his elbows."

Picard didn't allow himself the chuckle Riker'd been looking for. "I've discussed this with Spock, and now I'll discuss it with you." He stopped and Riker did as well.

"Sir?"

"We can't know what T'sart has planned, but it is something. I'm sure he doesn't intend to stay under our control. But he must. He cannot be allowed to escape."

Riker nodded slowly. "Aye, sir."

"Will . . ." The captain rarely called his first officer by his given name. When he did, it was usually more serious than light. "I mean he can't be allowed to escape. At any cost."

They were silent a moment, and Riker understood. "Aye, sir. Any cost."

Picard nodded once. "There's a reason I gave that order to Spock as well, Number One. I need you to help secure our passage through Romulan space. I have no intention of doing as T'sart suggests and killing any Romulan ship we'd come across while their shields are down."

"What did you have in mind?"

"Well, Mr. Riker," Picard said as the lift doors opened and they stepped out onto the bridge, "you're going to take a runabout and buy us some insurance. Mr. Spock knows of a Romulan unmanned subspace relay station. The Romulans keep supplies there, not unguarded, but completely automated. One of those supplies, an element they use in their plasma conduits, could be added to our nacelle exhaust. Romulan sensors might mistake that as a Romulan warp signature."

"Might and could. Are we sure of anything?" Riker asked.

Picard smiled lightly. "We know where the relay station itself is."

"Comforting. I've never even heard of this sort of element."

"Barantium. It's a secret use. One we've been saving for a rainy day."

"And it's monsoon season."

"Indeed. We'll head into Klingon space, and rendezvous back here in fourteen hours."

Will Riker pulled in a deep breath and pushed it out slowly. "Well, I hope I have a few tricks up *my* sleeve."

The captain nodded. "You do. Mr. Data and Counselor Troi, both of whom have some experience with Romulan computer systems, will accompany you. You'll use the codes T'sart has provided us, to scan cloaked ships. Unless you stumble across a dead zone yourself, you should at least get there."

Riker looked toward Data at the science station, and down to Deanna Troi on the lower bridge. "And if those codes to show us the cloaked ships are false?"

Picard pressed his lips into a thin line. "Keep your

heads down." Then, more somberly, the captain took his first officer's shoulder in one hand and gripped him tightly. "This is important, Will. I don't trust T'sart, and I don't trust his assurances. We need this barantium if we're to make it all the way through Romulan space."

"Then you'll have it, sir," Riker said, and gave an assuring nod. "You have my word."

Picard smiled weakly. "And I'll hold you to it."

Chapter Sixteen

Enterprise Runabout *Kaku*
Romulan Space
Sector 18

"HOW MUCH FARTHER?" Deanna Troi glanced at the navigation console, searching for her own answer.

Will Riker turned toward her, checking a few readouts as he swiveled in his chair. "You're not going to be like a kid on a long trip, are you?"

She smiled back at him.

"Hard to tell," he said. "We've had to change course three times now."

"At least T'sart was honest about the scanning code," Deanna said. "We can see cloaked warbirds soon enough to avoid them."

Riker's brow furrowed, and Deanna felt a few differ-

151

ent emotions radiate toward her. He was concerned, and also somewhat frustrated. "Who knows what he's being honest about? I'm still not trusting him. You try reading him at all?"

"Mm-hmm. I'm still feeling a bit arrogant from the encounter."

Riker smiled and nudged the arm of her chair. "Not used to reading that emotion?"

Absentmindedly altering one of the monitors above her, Deanna smiled playfully. "Only when I'm with you."

From his station aft, Data cleared his throat.

"Something, Commander?" Riker asked.

"May I be blunt, sir?"

Deanna felt Riker's amusement as he answered. "You can give it a try, Data."

"I can never tell if you two are arguing or flirting."

She and Riker exchanged a long glance where silence dominated until Riker finally said, "You'll have to work that one out on your own."

Data nodded his head to one side. "Perhaps later, sir. I—" The android stopped and turned toward his console so quickly that Deanna was taken aback. "I am reading a vessel decloaking," Data said, his hands suddenly in a quick dance over his controls.

Now Riker was rigid in his seat, all evidence of relaxation gone from his emotional broadcast. "Raise shields," he ordered. "For all the good it'll do us against a warbird. Put 'em on screen."

By this time Deanna, too, had buried herself in scanners and sensors. But she also took a moment to look up on the main viewscreen. "It's a—" She stammered.

She'd thought she'd be able to identify it. She'd famil-
iarized herself with all the files *Enterprise* had on Romulan fleet ships. "I don't know what that is."

"Data, check configuration against known schematics of *any*—"

"Checking now, sir." The android bent over his console.

"You recognize that *at all?*" Riker asked her.

Deanna shook her head. "It doesn't even look Romulan."

"It is not Romulan," Data said, turning to them from
his station. "The design is Galbutian. The Romulan
government purchased several of these ships from the
neutral Galbutians. They are commonly used to haul
large quantities of cargo between star systems. Lacking
stasis holds, they are not used for organic matter or un-
stable elements."

"What are they used for?

Data gave his version of a shrug, a small motion he
made with his eyebrows. "I would assume mostly stable waste removal."

"It's a garbage scow?" Riker was incredulous for a
moment. Deanna felt that, then she felt something common from him. Not an emotion, per se. It was something she simply felt when she knew he was . . . well,
for lack of a better term, "plotting."

"That is one way to put it, sir."

"It should be weaponless," Riker said. "Then again,
it should be cloakless, too."

"Yes, sir. The vessel is hailing us."

Eyes widening, Riker paused a moment, then
shrugged. "Well . . . put them on."

"Hello! You are Federation, yes?"

Riker nodded slowly. "Right." He turned to Deanna and whispered. "He's talking without a translator."

"I noticed," Deanna said.

"And you are?" Riker asked.

"I, Tobin." The Romulan smiled. Deanna noticed his hair was disheveled and he appeared not to have shaved in a few days. *"Captives. Okay?"*

Riker didn't answer. He whispered to Deanna. "Is he trying to take us captive?"

Her turn to shrug. "I'm not sure. Whatever he's saying, he seems very happy about it."

"Captive? Okay?" Tobin repeated. *"You see me, yes?"*

"Yeah, we see you." Riker said.

The Romulan smiled widely.

"He seems very . . . odd, sir," Data said.

Letting out a light whistle, Riker nodded agreement. "No weapons on his ship, right, Data?"

"No, sir. A lot of plastiform rubbish, however."

"I don't suppose there's any of the plasma conduit material we're looking for? Barantium?"

"Not that I detect, sir."

"Captive! Now!" Tobin yelled, but continued to smile. Was he pleased he'd "captured" the runabout? And just how had he? He had no weapons, just a cloak. And why a cloak on that ship? And why had they not seen through that cloak as they had all the others? Deanna entertained all these questions and more, and felt Riker was probably doing the same.

Finally she gave voice to the real threat. "What are we going to do? All he has to do is tell others we're here."

"Has he sent any messages, Data?" Riker asked.

"No, sir."

"Shields?"

"His shields are down, sir."

Riker chewed on his lower lip a quick moment, then made a decision and nodded to himself. "Beam him over."

Deanna touched his arm. "Pardon?"

"He's the only one aboard, he has yet to tell anyone we're here, I'd say now is the time."

She sighed, unable to argue with that. "All right."

"I'm glad I have your approval." Riker looked back toward Data, "Lock on and energize."

The android tapped at the console to his left. "Energizing."

In the aft transporter alcove, light and sparkle quickly formed and then dissipated, leaving a short, somewhat chubby Romulan behind.

"Hello there! I am Tobin! Captive!"

The Romulan rushed onto the deck, past Data and toward Riker. All three Starfleeters barely had time to bring their phasers up before Tobin grabbed Riker and hugged him.

Phaser at his side, Riker pushed the smiling Tobin off him. "Uh . . . we surrender?"

Klingon Warship *Qulric*
Klingon Space
Malinga Sector

"Sir."

Kalor awoke slowly, jarringly, at the sound of his

aide's voice. He glanced toward the doorway and saw Parl's face, half hidden in the dim light. Squinting at the chronometer across the room, Kalor didn't need to wonder why it felt as if he'd slept only half an hour—that was how long it had actually been.

The governor imagined himself eviscerating Parl. He'd left orders not to be disturbed.

"What?" Kalor barked.

"There is something on the scanners. Something you should see."

"If you woke me for a sensor ghost . . ." Kalor slid off his bed, groaning as his bones creaked in pain.

His first officer held out his robe. "Governor, I would not—"

"Stop sniveling, Parl." Kalor waved off the robe and walked into the corridor in his underclothes. He glared up at the taller, thinner man, and allowed the younger warrior to steady him as he walked. "What is so important?"

"It is the *Enterprise,* sir. They are hailing us."

Kalor stopped a moment, then continued walking toward the lift. "Us? The *Enterprise,* here? You're drunk again, aren't you?"

Lowering his head, Parl nodded. "Yes, sir, a little. But I am not mistaken." He handed the governor of Malinga a data padd. "Look, it is a Federation Battle Cruiser. *Enterprise.* That message we received, sir, the Romulan buoy. Could it have been true?"

The governor stared at the data a moment. "What were you drinking?"

"Sir, I swear, I am not that drunk. Do you not see it as well?"

"I do," Kalor said, sighing heavily. "What were you drinking, Parl?"

"Bloodwine, sir."

The governor cleared his rough throat. "Get me some."

U.S.S. Enterprise, NCC 1701-E
Klingon Space
Malinga Sector

"Captain, the governor of Malinga is answering our hail."

Picard stood, straightening his tunic. "Ambassador Spock, you may want to stand out of view."

The Vulcan nodded, and once he'd stood and moved to the extreme starboard aft of the bridge, Picard motioned toward the main viewer. "On screen."

"Aye, sir."

"This is Captain Jean-Luc Picard of the Federation Starship—"

The large Klingon on the main screen waved the introduction off. *"No need, Captain. Not only is your reputation known, of course, but I remember you."*

"Governor Kalor. Of course. Thank you." *I think.* Picard gave his best diplomatic nod, as Klingons tended not to respect a toothy smile. This needed to be handled with great care. Much hinged upon the specific series of events Picard had planned. And at the moment, he had no backup plan.

"Your destination within the Empire?" Kalor asked,

appearing somewhat disinterested as he gazed nonchalantly off screen and then back.

There was something, a flicker in Kalor's eye, perhaps, or just the extra care with which Kalor was being so studied in his devil-may-care attitude, but Picard sensed an agenda. An agenda larger than just meeting the *Enterprise* as treaty stipulated. "Our destination is the seventh planet of the W'lett-Kard system."

Kalor nodded pleasantly. Well, pleasantly for a Klingon—he didn't sneer. *"Quite remote. Purpose?"*

"We're transporting a scientist from a subspace research station there." Picard was sure to maintain an even tone. If Kalor was digging, he'd come up dry. And since long-range subspace communications had broken down for the Klingons as well, there would be no way to check Picard's story. "He's to accompany us to Starbase 10, a meeting to investigate the loss of subspace communications throughout the quadrant."

Taking a padd from one of his men, looking at it, then handing it back, Kalor paused a moment. *"I don't have authorization for that . . . but I'm sure that's a mere oversight. Sometimes we're overlooked this far out."*

"Yes, this *is* off the beaten path, isn't it?" Picard almost chuckled.

"Indeed. In fact, I'm surprised to see that your course took you into this sector at all. Not much out here, except some far-off colonies and the Romulan border." Kalor leaned back in his command chair, waiting.

"We had to divert our course due to an ion storm," Picard answered the implied question, but not too quickly.

"Of course," Kalor said. *"I would be honored to escort you to the boundary of my jurisdiction."*

He knows something's not right, Picard thought, *though how could he?* "Oh, a gracious offer indeed, but that won't be necessary."

Kalor leaned forward. *"I insist."*

"In that case . . ." Picard waved his hand, gesturing his assent. He continued the slightest of smiles, but the rock in his gut was pulling down any hope that Kalor didn't suspect something out of the ordinary.

"I will, of course, need to inspect your ship for any contraband cargo," Kalor said.

"We're carrying no cargo."

"Hmmm . . ." The Klingon commander looked off-screen and then back again. *"I seem unable to scan within your ship to determine that."*

"Standard Starfleet procedure—" Picard said evenly.

"Oh, I more than understand, Captain. More than understand. And you understand that I need to know your cargo, if any, and what it might be."

Picard nodded.

"It's just a regulation," Kalor continued. *"A duty I'm sworn to, you see. A formality, really. Perhaps all that is really needed is a good meal between our officers. A small tour of your ship and some good food, eh?"*

"Of course, we'd be honored." The captain felt his muscles tense, from his shoulders to his calves. He worked to make sure that didn't show in his posture.

Much more relaxed, Kalor moved his girth forward in his seat. *"Ambassador Worf has served on your ship, Captain. You have served as Arbiter of Succession for*

*the previous chancellor. We have a relationship with
you. We do not really need to inspect your cargo holds.
But I'm sure your replicator has some amazing Klingon
dishes, eh? Yes?"*

"It would be a rare pleasure to host you for dinner
and a brief tour. But we *are* on a schedule."

"Of course, Captain," Kalor said. *"I understand. I
look forward to seeing you. Kalor out."*

The screen flashed back to the serene starscape view.

Picard turned toward Spock as the Vulcan stepped
down to the command chair. "If not about T'sart, he
knows something."

"I concur," Spock said gravely.

"Mr. Spock?"

"Yes, Captain?"

"We need a plan."

Klingon Warship *Qulric*
Klingon Space
Malinga Sector

"You have a plan, Governor?"

Kalor halfheartedly backhanded his aide on the side
of the head. "Of course, Parl. We will have dinner, and
while Picard and I talk, you will find his special cargo."

Either confused from the light blow to his head, or
more likely by life in general, Parl's brows drew together. "We will not simply beam on an assault
team?"

Kalor hit him again. "You want to try to take a Federation starship by force? Alone? *That* Federation starship?"

"No, Governor."

"To do anything, we will have to wait for our two sister ships to return." Kalor stepped down from the command chair, stroked his beard, and turned toward the bridge lift. "Sober up, Parl. That's an order."

"Yes, Governor," Parl said as he followed. "But why wait until after dinner to distract Picard?"

"Because, Parl," Kalor said with a sigh, "I'm hungry."

Chapter Seventeen

**U.S.S. Enterprise, NCC 1701-E
Klingon Space
Malinga Sector**

"Where is he?"

Kalor's tone was less angry than it was disgusted. He'd been relatively silent through dinner, and now Picard understood why.

They sat alone in the captain's dining area, Kalor on one side of the table, Picard on the other.

The captain took in a breath and opened his mouth to answer.

With a raised hand, Kalor stopped Picard from beginning whatever it was he'd planned to say. "Don't, Picard. Do not dishonor either of us with subterfuge."

He wasn't intending to lie to Kalor, and anger at the

insinuation flushed his face. Hopefully it didn't look like embarrassment. Even though that, too, was a feeling. He agreed with Kalor's disgust—T'sart was a disgusting man who'd done disgusting things.

"How?" Picard asked finally, his voice a low gravel.

"No, you tell me—"

Picard didn't yell. He didn't wave off Kalor's comment. He didn't pound anything. He simply hammered the Klingon with a glare, and spoke with slow intensity. "I want to know how."

Curling his lips in thought, Kalor seemed to consider an answer. He would lie, or he would tell the truth, Picard knew, but he would answer no matter what. And it was difficult for Picard not to sympathize. How many lies had he already told Kalor?

"The Romulans," the Klingon said finally, and Picard wasn't sure if the distaste in his voice was a holdover from his thoughts of T'sart, or just because he'd had to deal with an enemy such as the Romulans. True, the two empires had allied with the Federation and each other during the Dominion War, but treaties couldn't eliminate a century of acrimony.

"You can't have him," Picard said, and took a sip of the tea in front of him. The water didn't take the dryness from his throat. That was there not from thirst, but from irritation. At Kalor, yes, but mostly at T'sart.

"How can you protect him, Picard?" Kalor asked.

"My duty—" Picard began.

"I know about duty," the Klingon barked. "There is no moral duty to protect something like him."

Picard huffed angrily. "My duty is to justice. Not to

revenge." He didn't want to have this argument, not now, not here. There was a more important ticking clock—the dead zone problem—pounding in the back of his mind. That was one reason he didn't want to have the discussion. The other was: he could have easily been on Kalor's side. *There's more here,* Picard kept telling himself.

"I want to see him," Kalor demanded before Picard could formulate an explanation.

The captain shook his head. "You can't have him." Picard could only begin to imagine the tortures a Klingon court verdict would render on T'sart. Which isn't to say the man didn't deserve it, but if he had the answer to stopping the dead zones . . .

Kalor scoffed. "I don't want him. I'm not foolish enough to believe you'd just turn him over to me and then be on your way."

"Then why do you want to see him?"

Leaning forward, Kalor's stomach pushed his empty dinner plate forward, clinking it against his empty glass of bloodwine. "Because . . . it is owed me. It is owed every Klingon."

Picard was silent. T'sart did have a debt to repay, to the Klingons and to many, many more.

"Do you know what he did?" Kalor continued. "Do I need to tell you how much death he's caused? How much suffering?"

"No," Picard whispered.

"To kill a Klingon with disease . . ." Kalor thrust himself harshly back into his chair. "It is the ultimate dishonor."

The captain glanced away, then quickly back. He knew Kalor, and Kalor knew him, but showing weakness to any Klingon was a mistake. They only understood the empathy another might have so far as they could use it to their advantage. Picard let his eyes become stone-set and cool.

"I want to see him," Kalor said.

"To what end?"

Kalor paused, then finally said, "You owe me this."

Picard shook his head. "I owe you nothing. If anyone has a debt here—"

The Klingon pounded an open hand on the table. "Paid in full, Picard! If only by mere fact that I do not call other Klingons here to take this *petaQ* by force."

"There *is* more to this," Picard barked back. "I've salvaged your honor before. Shouldn't you honor me now if I ask it?"

Kalor looked away, remembering something he'd rather not. "I've not forgotten what you did." He turned back, shaking his head, his jowls quivering in anger. "But what you've done now does not just dishonor yourself, or Klingons. It dishonors all those who live."

"Kalor, T'sart is important—"

"So is the honor of the dead. So is justice, which you claim you have a duty to." The Klingon straightened, seeming to stand taller than his actual height. "I will not listen to Federation explanations. I want to see him."

Picard tried to weigh the possible ramifications of a short confrontation. Would it scare T'sart? Probably not. Would it anger him? Most certainly. Could he afford that? Yes. In fact, he'd somewhat enjoy it. Would

Kalor try to hurt the Romulan? Probably not. He would know that to be futile.

"I'll give you five minutes," Picard said finally. "With myself and my guards present."

"I want to see him alone."

The captain stood. "Then I'll have you escorted off my ship."

Kalor nodded. "Five minutes."

Enterprise Runabout *Kaku*
Romulan Space
Sector 18

"He does not have a weapon, sir." Data stood a few meters away from their Romulan captive, a tricorder in one hand and phaser in the other.

The Romulan smiled at Data, then at Riker. "I no have weapon. Surrender now? Captive?"

"Is he really cheerful, or is this an act?" Riker asked Deanna out the side of his mouth.

"Definitely very cheerful," she said.

Data holstered his tricorder, but not his phaser. "If I may, sir, I think he wants us to take him captive."

Nodding, Riker motioned for the Romulan to take a seat near one of the unused monitor consoles. "Sit?" he asked, then turned to Deanna. "Why isn't he speaking his own language?"

Taking a chair herself, Deanna shrugged. "Ask him."

A smile turned the corners of Riker's lips up. Of course. Ask. "Right." He turned to the Romulan.

"Why are you speaking our language without a translator?"

For a moment, the Romulan's face went blank, quizzical. Then he smiled again. "Your language, good. I speak well, praise myself, no?"

"Do you have a name?" Deanna asked.

"Yes," the Romulan said after brief thought.

Deanna leaned forward in her seat and smiled charmingly. She could still melt any man with that look, Riker thought. "What *is* your name?"

The Romulan looked confused and slowly shook his head. "No. 'What' is not my name."

Thumb and forefinger pressing into the bridge of his nose, Riker definitely felt a headache coming on. "Would you *please* speak your language. *Yours.* We want to understand you better. Okay?"

"I understand well, praise myself, okay?"

Deanna chuckled. "That *is* very Romulan, isn't it? Self-praise?"

Riker sighed. "Do you want to help here?"

"Sure." Deanna turned and stood. "Computer, translate my next sentence into Romulan standard language and play it back."

"Acknowledged."

"I understand you're very enthused about being here, and we're glad to see you, too. But if you'll speak your language, we'll speak ours, and we'll be able to understand one another much better through our universal translators. All right?"

Still radiating that smile, but with maybe a little disappointment behind his eyes, the Romulan nodded, then spoke. This time, he was speaking his native language, and the translator kicked in immediately. "Certainly. My apologies for any inconvenience. I try to practice whenever I get the chance. You're Federation, correct? I recognized your vessel as Federation design. Starfleet as well. I am very pleased to see you, but what are you doing out here?"

Relieved, Riker sighed. *That is* much *better.* "We were wondering the same about you. Especially wondering why you have a garbage truck that cloaks?"

A bit confused, the Romulan cocked his head backward a bit. " 'Truck'? What is that word? It translated to transport, but I've never heard it before."

Interesting. He was listening to both the original and the translation. Not an easy task. Riker was so used to the translator, he didn't even hear an alien's normal speech anymore.

"You're listening to the translation and our speech as well?" Deanna asked. She must have been just as surprised. Or she read the thought from Riker's mind. He was never quite sure with her.

"Linguistics and dialects are a hobby," the Romulan said.

"Do you have a name?" Data asked. Riker noted his phaser was still leveled at the seated Romulan. Good.

"My name is Tobin. Can you tell me what a truck is?" He said truck with a more Romulan accent. Like "trook."

"A truck is . . . a transport. A vehicle," Deanna answered.

While she and Data were being friendly, Riker was

being concerned. "Excuse me, Tobin. I'd like to know how you managed to get a cloak for your ship."

"I'm escaping," Tobin said cheerfully. "I'm coming to the Federation. Defecting. This is the least-used transport route. I saw your ion trail, and when I thought it looked Federation, I came back."

Riker chewed the inside of his lower lip a bit. He wasn't sure he believed Tobin. Space is very big, and that they had happened to meet up seemed more than coincidence. There was nothing Riker could think of that made their ion trail look specifically Federation. Not since they'd taken steps to mask it.

He almost asked Deanna if she thought the Romulan was lying, but Riker knew her well enough that if she did, she'd mention it. He also knew that Tobin's exuberance was probably overwhelming all other senses.

"That doesn't answer how you managed to get a cloak for a nonmilitary vessel. Were you, or are you, a member of the Romulan military?"

"No, certainly not." Tobin's expression became sour.

That could certainly be an act, Riker thought. "I'm not sure I believe you. If you're not military, how did you get the cloak?"

Tobin didn't hesitate, and the bitter edge to his features disappeared. "My cousin is involved in warbird construction. It is not hard to get the proper parts if you know what to replicate. The hard part is generating enough power. Only a larger vessel, like the size of mine, will have room for a warp core big enough."

"You're not using a quantum singularity method of

warp manipulation?" Deanna asked. Riker has almost forgotten her experience with Romulan warp technology.

"No, that isn't available on many older ships. I have a standard matter/antimatter warp core." It seemed Tobin was willing to discuss anything with interest and at some length. He was very open. So far.

"Very interesting," Riker said. "And convenient."

"Convenient?" Data asked.

"Something's wrong with all this," Riker said, and he wasn't afraid to let Tobin hear it. "I don't know what, but something smells fishy."

Their Romulan guest got that quizzical look on his face again, and his brows knitted. "What is 'fishy'?"

"I don't know yet, Mr. Tobin," Riker said. "But I intend to find out."

U.S.S. Enterprise, NCC 1701-E
Klingon Space
Malinga Sector

"Am I to inspect the trash before you discard it now, Picard?"

Kalor seethed at T'sart's comment. At his snide Romulan tone and arrogant Romulan face.

His blood hot with hate and anger, Kalor felt his muscles tense for the kill. But he could not kill him here, not as he wanted. He wanted to feel T'sart's throat crushed in his bare hands. He wanted to press out the devil's last breath of life so he could spit into it. But first he wanted to hurt the Romulan in ways no other being had ever been hurt. Kalor would invent new ways, if necessary.

"Hold your tongue, Romulan," the Klingon spat as he let his hatred burn through his eyes and into T'sart.

"Why did you bring him here?" T'sart asked Picard. "Are you showing me off like a trophy? I'll remind you I'm here because I wish to be."

That was the largest crime of all. That Picard had this monster where all of the Klingon Empire, all of the quadrant, wanted him, and he wasn't even in the brig. He was in his own quarters, being pampered by a dishonorable Federation. Picard had the Romulan within his grasp, and all he did was shake the villain's hand.

Kalor stood straight before T'sart, squeezed the buckle on his belt, and nodded with satisfaction. "I've seen enough."

"Hm? You don't want a souvenir voice-stamped holograph?" T'sart mocked.

Picard motioned toward the door. "Enough, from both of you."

The Klingon turned on his heel and stalked out of the room. The guards stayed behind, but Picard followed.

Once in the corridor, Kalor noticed Picard shaking his head.

"Satisfied?" the starship captain asked.

Kalor smiled inwardly, but had not a chance to answer. The sound of distant explosions, then alert klaxons, filled the ship.

Damn you, Parl! Kalor cursed to himself. *You are too early!*

"La Forge to Captain Picard."

Picard slapped at his comm badge, a light film of perspiration glinting off his head. "Report, La Forge!"

"Kalor's ship fired on us, Captain! Warp power is off-line. Shields are up now, but compromised dorsal, aft and starboard. And we have six Klingon birds-of-prey on an intercept vector."

As his subordinate spoke, Picard only glared at Kalor. A stare not unlike the one he had just visited upon T'sart.

"Signal battle stations. Then get to Engineering, Mr. La Forge. Leave the bridge to Spock. I'll be right there.

"Aye, sir."

"And get security down here. Governor Kalor is under arrest."

Chapter Eighteen

PICARD HAD BEEN FOOLISH, something he most often wasn't. Being so, and the captain of a starship, put many people in peril. Being so today, with all that was happening, put the galaxy in peril. He wasn't in the best of moods about that.

In his anger, Picard almost had Kalor taken to the makeshift brig. Then he thought better, and ordered that the Klingon governor merely be flanked by two security guards. Sad but true—he might need Kalor still.

"Captain on the bridge." Spock's voice was clear as he stepped down from the command chair. He was wearing a standard issue uniform now, with the appropriate rank. A Starfleet captain before Picard was even born, he wondered if the Vulcan had the urge to stay in the center seat. Picard would have, even if it weren't his command.

"Status." He stepped down to the command deck as Spock handed the captain a padd and moved toward the monitor station next to the captain's chair. Kalor was held on the upper deck by the guards.

"Shields are operable. We are on impulse power. Warp power is still off-line."

"Hail Kalor's ship," Picard ordered.

Shapiro nodded, already having the connection ready. "On screen."

Picard looked at the Klingon on the main viewer and decided greetings were unnecessary. "You are?" he demanded.

The Klingon didn't flinch. *"Parl. Second in command."*

The captain nodded and waved the Klingon off. "We have Governor Kalor in custody. Warn the approaching ships off."

Parl shook his head slowly. *"I can't do that, Captain."* He wasn't angry. In fact, for a Klingon he was rather mellow.

Not feeling mellow himself, Picard nodded for Kalor's guards to bring him forward a step. Roughly. "Tell him."

"No." Kalor looked to Parl and shook his head.

"Fine. Mr. Chamberlain, lock our phasers on the Klingon vessel."

Lieutenant Chamberlain's hands dabbed at the tactical board. "Phasers locked."

"Disruptors locked?" Parl asked someone off screen.

"Locked," was the gruff reply.

A game of chicken. Picard could win it, easily, despite being warp-disabled.

"There are six more, Picard," Kalor said. He knew his ship could be taken. And he knew it was worth the sacrifice. The *Enterprise* against six other ships, however, that was another matter.

The captain nodded and thumbed a panel on the arm of his command chair. "Picard to Engineering."

"La Forge here."

"Mr. Spock gave me a report, Mr. La Forge. If I read this right, it's similar to the damage from that overload a few weeks ago, correct?"

There was the very slightest of delays before Geordi's response. *"Aye, sir. About two days to repair those circuits, sir."*

"Understood. Picard out."

Calculated risk, Picard thought. But he'd been taking too much of a backseat to the events of the last few days. He'd let T'sart chart *Enterprise*'s course, and had almost let Kalor. No more.

"I'm not asking you to surrender your ship," Kalor said. "I would not dishonor you that way"

Picard scoffed. "You *have* dishonored me. And yourself."

"As you have, by bringing that *petaQ* here!" Kalor broke forward from his guards and leaned over the rail toward Picard. "By having him at all!"

"The dead zones—"

Kalor spat. "I care *not* about them, Picard! I am not a scientist. I am a soldier, and a creature of duty."

The captain rose slowly, turning, but not ordering the main viewer off. Let Parl watch, and listen. "You have no duty to the lives of other Klingons?"

"I have a duty to avenge the deaths of those Klingons who were killed without honor. At *that* monster's hand." The word "that" was punctuated with a growl and a fist pounding on the guardrail.

There were not many ways to dishonor a Klingon in death, but T'sart had perfected at least one: disease. Genetic warfare, outlawed by most Alpha Quadrant governments, was still researched by most, usually defensively. T'sart was a master practitioner of the offensive.

In more ways than one.

Picard turned back to the main viewer. "Parl, is it?"

Parl nodded.

"You have until we repair our damage to retreat outside our weapons range. After that, Federation/Klingon treaties will be ignored."

"Understood," Parl said calmly.

"You're staying here," Picard said to Kalor. "Mr. Spock, take the governor into my ready room. Explain the situation to him."

Spock nodded. "Of course, Captain."

The guards tugged at Kalor's arms. "What is this? I do not need a Vulcan to explain anything to me. What are you doing?"

Pushing out a frustrated huff, Picard mumbled, "Hoping you can be reasoned with."

Romulan Warbird *Makluan*
Romulan/Klingon border
Sector 22

Folan looked out onto a starscape with stars not her own. She had no friends among the people around her on the bridge, or the suns about her, and she was feeling the loneliness of that fact.

Her ship was now mostly repaired, using backups and bypasses, which could collapse with another battle. Perhaps without one. Long-range communications were still down, and that meant even if she had wanted more help, she could not ask for it.

As for her crew . . . she was fooling herself calling them hers, as much as she was in calling the ship hers.

Medric, the person most likely to take command from her at his first opportunity, had worked silently for hours. So had the others. Folan had not wanted to leave the bridge, lest what was silence became whispers, and then chants against her authority.

If T'sart was now dead, as she hoped, then her authority would not be questioned. But she'd not heard from the Klingons, and at this point thought it unlikely she would. They'd either ignored her message as treachery, or heeded it but would not respect her with a return response. There was the chance Medric was wrong, and the *Makluan* could not receive a message as well as send one. But . . . why would he lie about something so easily checked? She was being paranoid.

So, other than looking over her shoulder, what should she do? She wanted to sleep . . . sleep and not wake up for years. Sleep, and when she did finally awake, be in her bed, a child, in her mother's house. She . . .

. . . needed to stop thinking like that.

Enterprise was where T'sart was. Where Picard was. What Folan needed, she decided, was to find the *Enterprise* herself. She would confirm T'sart's death, or cause it, and achieve Picard's as well.

Deciding on that course of action, she then asked herself the questions she should have posed before. Why Klingon space, and why now? The Klingons hated T'sart more than anyone, save perhaps Folan herself.

Something was out of place. Folan wanted to know what.

"Medric." She bounded out of the command chair and toward the centurion's station. "Calculate *Enterprise*'s current position based on last known location and trajectory."

He looked up. "I know how to extrapolate a current position. Why?"

"Do it," Folan snapped.

The man clicked at his console, and then pointed to a graph on a monitor. "Klingon space. Malinga sector."

"Helm," Folan called, turning. "Set a course. Best possible speed to the Malinga sector."

Folan stepped back down to the command chair. She didn't watch Medric's glances at other crewman. But she felt them. And she worried.

U.S.S. Enterprise, NCC 1701-E
Klingon Space
Malinga Sector

It didn't take long for the other Klingon ships to arrive. When they had, Kalor's ship took *Enterprise* in tow and they headed toward the Malinga colony, where Kalor sat as governor.

In that brief time, Picard had taken a few moments to discuss some options privately with La Forge. He went back to his ready room when Spock had finished explaining the entire situation to Kalor.

"You expect me to believe this, Picard? That this one animal is the only one who knows how to stop these dead zones?" Kalor's expression was full of anger and distrust.

Picard sighed and lowered himself into the chair behind his desk. "I don't even know that much. I *do* know that T'sart has more information on these dead zones than anyone in the Federation, and the data *does* suggest the source could be more toward Romulan space than anything else."

His anger still swirling but more controlled, Kalor balled his fists at his side. "Did you ever think the monster himself could be behind these death zones? That you could be an unwitting pawn in a Romulan scheme? Or just *his* scheme?"

The captain shared a quick glance with Spock. "Yes, the thought has occurred to us."

"Then why not assume that? It is much more likely, yes?"

"Indeed." Picard looked at something on his desk computer screen, then spun the monitor away. "And I'm not suggesting that's not most likely. But whether T'sart is behind these happenings, or simply understands them, he knows more than we do. And if his thinking me a pawn will get these phenomena stopped, then so be it."

In a gesture one didn't often see in a Klingon, Kalor both sighed and shrugged. "You're not usually a fool, Picard," he said, and there was a hint of "even if I sometimes am" in his tone. "But how do you know he's not better than you are in such games?"

"How do you know he is?" Picard said, and smiled slightly. But it was bravado. Picard wasn't sure at all. He leaned forward over the desk. "I need your help, Kalor."

"My duty was to kill him, and that I have."

Picard felt his brow furrow. *"Have?* Past tense?"

"A virus. The same one he used to kill seven thousand Klingons and cause another forty thousand to suffer, myself included."

The captain stood. "Then there is a cure?"

Kalor shook his head. He sounded neither satisfied nor victorious. *Was* it just duty to him? "The virus has been genetically re-engineered to kill only him."

Picard shook his head. When had this happened? "How?"

"Beamed into him." Kalor removed his belt buckle and laid it on the table. "Small transporter transponder. It focused our beam to coordinate within his bloodstream when I got close enough."

The captain angrily shoved the transponder off the table. "Ignorant—" He slapped at his comm badge. "Picard to Dr. Crusher. Get T'sart to sickbay. Immediately."

"Aye, sir. Injury?"

"Virus. Full work-up, Doctor."

"On my way. Crusher out."

Kalor stood and Picard saw the guard at his door tense. Picard shook his head and the guard regained his composure.

"There is no cure, Picard."

The captain sighed heavily. "You'd better hope we can find one, or we're all dead."

Chapter Nineteen

U.S.S. Enterprise, NCC 1701-E
Klingon Space
Malinga Sector

"NASTY LITTLE VIRUS." Beverly Crusher huffed out an angry breath as she dropped the data padd on the table in front of T'sart. The Romulan stopped it from clattering around the desk.

Picard knew her well. She'd wanted it to clatter, liked to make noise when she was angry. It was her release, and she was probably annoyed that the Romulan had interrupted that.

"Thank you," he said, smiling in a manner neither cheerful nor sneering. "You have a keen eye for workmanship."

Sickbay was empty of patients, and Picard had asked

any others to exit. He and T'sart sat at Beverly's desk. The good doctor hovered over her not-so-good patient.

"If only it were the same as yours," she said, moving to his side, first scanning him up, then down. "But your antidote won't work with this variety. It's specially coded to your DNA."

T'sart nodded, as if listening to a piece of music he was well familiar with and was noting the chords had remained the same. "That will mean an exceedingly long duration before death."

"But not before symptoms arise," Beverly said, moving a long strand of red hair that had fallen before her eyes. "Painful symptoms."

T'sart smiled, more a ghoulish smirk than anything else. "I see your Klingon pets hadn't the skill to change enough of the virus."

The doctor closed her tricorder and put the hand scanner away. "They had enough. This *will* kill you."

T'sart shrugged elaborately. "Eventually, we all die."

"How long?" Picard asked Beverly.

She slid into her desk chair and tapped at her computer console. "Depends on his metabolism. I may be able to slow it. He could help if he fasts. Perhaps a week. If we're lucky."

The Romulan chuckled darkly. "Preservation of my life, and 'if we're lucky.' There's something I don't hear every day."

"We're going to try to save your life, T'sart. We'll do everything we can." Picard leaned toward him. "But now you'll have to tell us everything you know. Everything you've left out, and it's a great deal more, I'm sure."

Leaning back, T'sart breathed in slowly through his nose, then back out. He folded his hands across his stomach, steepling his fingers in a motion Picard considered rather stately and Vulcan. "It is a great deal indeed, Picard."

He wasn't sure if T'sart would speak truly. He thought he might, then in the next moment knew he wouldn't. "Tell us."

"Why? So you can save the galaxy? Without me in it, of what worth is the galaxy?"

Beverly harrumphed. "There's a sick thought."

"He's being quite serious." Spock's voice.

Picard turned to see the Vulcan was just through the doorway. He handed the captain a padd and then stood to the side, looking at T'sart.

"Yes, I'm very serious." T'sart was matter-of-fact. He continued reclining as he spoke. "Why should I care what becomes of the galaxy after my death?"

"Everything is about you?" Crusher asked.

T'sart nodded. "All the interesting things, yes."

"You won't help us." Picard wasn't asking a question.

"I'm not the helpful sort, Picard. I'll help myself. If that helps you, well, I'll have to live with that. But, 'live with' is the key. If I'm not alive to enjoy it . . . then I'm also not alive to have the problem that needs solving."

"A logical argument," Spock noted.

Beverly looked up at him, unintimidated by his cool Vulcan visage. "Then why isn't that *your* philosophy?"

Spock ignored the accusatory tone. "Because we have different core values. An argument can be logical while the premise is not. Vulcans prefer to have rational premises as well."

"Vulcans prefer to be arrogant and insufferable," T'sart said with a chuckle.

"You're to talk about arrogance?" Beverly wasted no bedside manner on T'sart.

"I, at least, gain pleasure from my own arrogance." He turns to Spock. "Do you?"

"There is nothing about you from which I gain pleasure," Spock said.

The Romulan grinned, probably sincerely. "You're extremely good at veiled insult."

Spock lowered his head slightly in a gesture neither of denial nor acceptance, something Picard had come to recognize as a Vulcan "if-you-say-so."

Suddenly the captain realized how lucky he was to have Spock on hand. What a vast array of knowledge and experience he could offer. Knowledge . . . experience . . . *abilities*. Picard turned in his chair toward the Vulcan. "I don't suppose . . ."

"A mind-meld?" Spock shook his head doubtfully. Amazing that he knew what Picard was considering. "I don't think that would satisfy our needs."

"Reason?" The captain knitted his brows.

"Because," T'sart offered, adjusting himself in his chair and straightening his tunic, "I'm a high-level Romulan official. It is mandatory that we are trained to be quite skilled in blocking mental attacks. Especially Vulcan mental attacks, considering the ease with which Romulan and Vulcan brain chemistry work together."

"We need to know what you know," Picard said.

T'sart smiled. "No one has that much time to learn."

The captain was unamused.

T'sart sighed, perhaps exasperated at his unadoring audience. "I'll help, Picard . . . and you'll help me. As long as I'm alive. You'll get no more than that." He turned to Beverly. "I'd get to work, if I were you."

Dr. Crusher pursed her lips, almost sneering as she handed him a tricorder. "I don't suppose you'd like to help?"

"For such a good cause?" T'sart smiled as he gracefully took the instrument. "But of course."

Kalor looked out Picard's office window and cradled his drink awkwardly at his side. Picard watched him, and wondered what he thought. Did he see his vessel's tractor beam reaching around *Enterprise* and wonder just what he'd done? Was there any awe at his own actions? Did he know how foolish he'd been?

"I want the cure for this disease," Picard said finally, breaking the long silence.

"I told you, there is none." Kalor's voice was thick and slow.

"Are you drunk?"

"No. Parl gets drunk."

"And you?"

Kalor chuckled. "I just drink."

Picard saw nothing fruitful if he pressed that, so he remained on task. "T'sart didn't have a cure for the Klingons, yet his virus killed only seven thousand."

"Only?" Kalor rasped.

"You understand what I mean, Kalor."

The Klingon nodded, but was still staring out the window. "We found a cure for ourselves. The virus is changed now."

"Give me the data on how." Picard stepped toward him. "Give me the antidote you created."

"You don't understand. Still. I cannot help you."

The captain took another step closer and reached out with his hand, turned Kalor toward him. "You're going to. Even if I have to force you."

Kalor snorted and took a swig of his drink. "Those are *my* ships that have you tractored and are towing you to *my* planet, Picard."

"Because I'm letting them, Kalor." He squeezed his fingers, not that Kalor would feel it through his thick tunic. "We could snap that tractor beam like a cobweb."

Kalor jerked away, spilling some of his drink as he did. "Then why don't you?"

"Because now isn't the time."

"You're waiting to repair yourself." The Klingon snorted again. "But we won't give you the two days—"

"The ship has been repaired for twenty minutes and will be ready for warp in another ten. But if T'sart dies, it may all be for nothing."

Kalor growled a low growl, more frustration than anger.

"Do you believe us?" Picard asked. "About the dead zones?"

The Klingon set his drink on the sill of the window and shook his head. "It's not a matter of believing you

187

or not. It's a matter of what is acceptable and expected. I cannot help you."

"I'm . . ." Picard hesitated. How much should he say? How much shouldn't he? "I'm not acting on orders here, Kalor."

"You?" Thick brows raised in surprise, Kalor almost laughed.

"We haven't time for orders, or what is appropriate. When a dead zone hits a populated area, people will die. Everyone dependent on advanced technology will die. And later, when even batteries and electricity won't work . . . We're talking about collapsing back to pre-industrial civilization. How many Klingon cities can last without power, Kalor?"

Kalor waved his hand dismissively. "Dramatic, but all we've had are a few ships fall into these zones. A few small incidents. How am I to know that this isn't all a trick? A plot by T'sart? They will end when he does, and that will be soon."

Ready to respond, Picard was interrupted by a comm signal.

He tapped at his comm badge. "Picard here."

"Spock here, Captain. We have a problem."

"On my way."

Kalor followed Picard onto the bridge. A security guard stood close by the Klingon as the captain strode toward the Vulcan and the science station.

"Something, Spock?"

"Based on readings I could recall from T'sart's data, I've begun scanning with a subspace resonance pulse. It has stopped echoing back to me."

Picard felt his face grow cold. "A dead zone?"

"Likely."

"Where?"

Spock pointed toward a monitor. "In our path, if we maintain this course."

"Intersect point?"

"Two minutes, fourteen seconds at current speed."

Picard swung around, pointing toward the helm as he made his way to the command chair. "Break the tractor beam." He slapped at his comm badge. "Bridge to Engineering. Geordi, I need warp power now."

"You got it, Captain."

"Helm, full reverse thrust."

"Aye, sir."

"Mr. Chamberlain, raise the Klingons." The captain pivoted toward Kalor. "Tell them to stop, now."

The Klingon commander hesitated. "I—are you sure?"

"Spock?"

"One minute, forty seconds," Spock said. "For the lead Klingon ship, fourteen seconds."

"Channel open," Chamberlain said from tactical.

"This is Kalor. All vessels, stop!"

Chamberlain shook his head. "They're not responding."

"Regulations," Kalor grumbled. "By taking me into custody, you've negated my command. They'll assume me under duress."

"Three Klingon ships now within probable dead zone," Spock called, bent over his scanner. "Falling out of warp."

"Fire phasers," Picard ordered. "Break that tractor! Fire!"

At Picard's command, a thin orange line traced a path toward the vessel in Parl's control. There was a bright explosion, a hum in the engines as they suddenly shifted acceleration, and a shudder as inertial dampers struggled to compensate.

"We're free," Spock said. "Decelerating from warp. We are still clear of the dead zone." He looked up from his sensors. "The Klingon ships were not as lucky."

"Can you raise them?"

Chamberlain again shook his head.

"Probably not on subspace channels," Spock offered.

Picard nodded. "Try nonsubspace communications."

"Aye, sir. Picking up something on radio frequencies."

"On speakers."

"—demanding any ship within reception contact Defense Force Command and Governor Kalor. Seventeen large vessels and forty smaller craft are stranded in orbit. All seven power generation plants on the surface have ceased functioning. Battery power will last only three more hours . . ."

"This . . . this is coming from my planet? From the Malinga colony?"

Picard nodded. "Only on battery backup . . ." he murmured. "When those fail, the matter/antimatter magnetic containment will collapse in each power plant—"

"Causing widespread destruction." Spock finished what Picard could not.

Kalor staggered toward Picard. "There's enough antimatter in those seven power plants to tear the atmosphere from the planet." His mouth was agape. "Nineteen million Klingons . . . we must get to them."

Picard spun toward the helm. "Distance?"

"Twenty billion kilometers."

The captain's gut felt tight. "Four light hours."

"Several days on impulse," Chamberlain mumbled from tactical.

"It doesn't matter," Picard said. "Twenty billion kilometers with radio communications . . . This transmission took four hours to get here. They've been dead an hour by now."

"And in three more hours," Kalor said, his voice gravel, "we will hear it happen to them."

Chapter Twenty

WITHIN AN HOUR IT HAD BEGUN. Those on the dying planet knew help wasn't coming. Transmissions, counter-transmissions: Klingon panic. Picard and his crew heard it all. The captain thought about taking it off the speakers, maybe just recording it. He couldn't. He listened. They all did. Helpless.

"Four vessels left in orbit. Seven were able to force themselves into space. The rest grew cold in orbit and died, asphyxiated." Static crackled throughout, but the tired Klingon voice was otherwise clear. Picard knew enough of the Klingon language to listen past the translator and he could hear the fatigue. The man was struggling,

mentally and physically. Probably a low-level communications officer on the planet. Kalor most likely had never met him. That mattered not. He was a ghost, and that thought was never far from anyone's thoughts. *"Station batteries useless for tractor beams. All available power is being channeled to antimatter containment. Limited batteries now available. We must have assistance. Too late for evacuation. If you can hear this and can respond . . . it is probably too late for that as well. Those with ships that could escape the gravity, have. If they can avoid the blast wave when the plants . . . if they can . . ."*

The man's voice trailed off. There was indistinct yelling in the background.

"He doesn't know what else to say," Kalor commented quietly.

Klingons with personal transmitters had clogged the frequencies. Most messages weren't pleas for help, but declarations about their deaths, for their families. Testimony of how honorable their bloodlines are . . . were . . . Somber self-epilogues, closing their lives with their own eulogies.

Real-time sensors wouldn't work within the dead zone, but light magnification, enhanced by computers, would show what occurred four hours ago, just as radio was picking up the broadcasts . . . from twenty billion kilometers away.

Soon enough, they'd see the planet go.

Kalor sighed. "I'd like some privacy to . . . talk to my ship, Picard."

Picard nodded. "My office."

* * *

Kalor felt heavy. He struggled to remain upright as he moved to the replicator in Picard's office and ordered the machine to give him another drink. He'd given up on bloodwine long ago and was downing a *chech'tluth*. He took the drink and shuffled over to Picard's desk, where he fell into the chair before the computer.

He took a long drag on the steaming drink as he tapped into the console to open a local communications channel.

His aide appeared on the monitor.

"Parl."

"Governor."

Parl had been under his command longer than anyone. He was Kalor's most trusted associate, and closest friend. They'd served together, been drunk together, chased women together, and fought together. They had the same strengths, and even the same weaknesses. "How drunk are you now, my friend?"

"Not nearly drunk enough, sir."

Kalor chuckled, but his chest was tight and it became a cough. "Neither am I." He coughed again, and took another sip of his drink. "We have been foolhardy."

A few lines of static snow broke the picture a moment, and Parl squinted. *"There was nothing we could have done to save the planet."*

"We succeeding in poisoning the monster," Kalor said. His voice sounded like gravel, and his throat was just as rough.

Parl's brows drew up and he spoke with deliberate slowness. *"That is . . . not a good thing?"*

Another cough before Kalor answered, and another gulp of his drink as well. "It is likely that he knows what causes these powerless areas in space. I don't trust him. Picard doesn't trust him. But if he can end these . . . and we have killed him . . ."

"*Honor—*" Parl began.

Kalor cut him off, gesturing with his free hand. "Honor is a harsh mistress, my friend." He sighed. "Picard has a plan to save our ship and the others. When the shockwave hits . . ." He noticed himself having trouble pronouncing the word for "shockwave," and he looked down at his drink. He took another slug on it, as if that might help. "He wants to transfer power to each ship. Have you draw energy right off his tractor beam. Enough to keep inertial dampers on-line."

"*We calculated that our dampers will fail. We are ready for that. At this point, death is a release . . .*"

"Picard will try nevertheless." Kalor sniffed. The room felt stuffy suddenly.

"*Picard is very trying,*" Parl said. It was an elegant pun for two men as drunk as Kalor and Parl were, and they both laughed.

"If Picard risks his ship for us, and he fails . . . then we will have failed again, and whether the monster lives or not, *Enterprise* will not be able to see their mission through. We cannot let that happen."

"*I understand, Governor.*"

Kalor raised his glass. It was empty, but he raised it anyway. "It has been an honor to serve with you, Parl."

"*And with you.*"

"Doctor." Picard greeted Beverly as he entered the sickbay laboratory.

"Captain." She nodded, looking quickly up from her computer screen and then back down. T'sart was at a different console. He didn't glance away.

"Any progress?" the captain asked.

She shook her head. "Nothing so far."

Picard walked to the edge of her desk and touched it lightly with one hand. "I hate to interrupt you, but we'll need your people to prepare for possible Klingon casualties."

T'sart now looked up. "Klingons?"

"You may need to call in extra shifts." Picard ignored the Romulan's obvious concern.

Beverly's head turned from T'sart to Picard. She felt the tension. "Aye, sir."

"Wait, Picard." T'sart now turned his chair completely toward the captain and away from the computer on which he'd been working. "Why are you taking on passengers?"

Ignoring the Romulan, Picard continued to talk directly to Beverly. "Seven Klingon ships are trapped in a nearby dead zone. Four light hours away, their planet's seven matter/antimatter reactors have lost containment."

"Klingon fools," T'sart spat. "They didn't have a contingency for blasting their cores into space if losing containment was imminent? They've destroyed their own planet."

"The subspace shockwave seems to have been easily dissipated by the dead zone," Picard continued, deliberately speaking only to the doctor. He lowered his voice just enough that it should be difficult for T'sart to hear without listening closely. "But the normal shockwave is on its way. With the ships in the dead zone, they haven't enough power for their inertial dampers."

"You're expecting the shockwave to push them out of the dead zone." T'sart frowned. "That it will, but at close to light speed. If they don't have inertial dampers, they'll be pounded to mush against their bulkheads. Having your doctor ready to fix broken legs won't help."

"We'll be going into the dead zone to retrieve them," Picard told her.

"You're insane," T'sart hissed.

Picard looked at him a moment. He was angry. That was the first time he'd really showed anything but smug arrogance or mild annoyance. T'sart was upset. At what? His own mortality? Then why wasn't he enraged that Kalor had poisoned him?

Unsure, the captain continued to ignore T'sart. "We'll be tractoring onto them. If we pour on the power, they should be able to collect some of that energy and transfer it to their inertial dampeners."

"That won't be enough," T'sart barked. "And you'll be weakened in the attempt. You're risking the destruction of this vessel for *them?*"

Staring at the Romulan for a long moment, Picard decided to finally speak directly to him. "Is that fear in your voice, T'sart? Surely not for our mission, not for the galaxy. Fear for yourself? I thought you didn't fear death."

"You're a fool, Picard."

"Why?" He took a step toward the angry Romulan. "Because I value life that's not my own?"

"It's not your life you're risking, but the lives of every living thing in this entire galaxy."

The more emotion that seethed into T'sart's voice, the more calm and matter-of-fact Picard made his own. "I don't believe it's an either/or situation. But your argument might be more persuasive if we didn't know exactly how much you cared for any life but your own: nothing. However . . . your fear of death is interesting, T'sart. I'll be sure to remember it."

They were silent for a time, until Picard's comm badge beeped.

"Spock to Picard."

He tapped his badge. "Picard here."

"Captain, we have a problem. The Klingons are using their thrusters to go deeper into the dead zone."

"I'll be right there." Picard nodded to Doctor Crusher. "Have sickbay ready," he told her, then turned and left.

Picard found Kalor still in the captain's ready room off the bridge, slumped in Picard's desk chair. "You want to explain what in hell your ships are doing?"

The Klingon looked up and squinted into the light. His face was flushed a bit purple and the flesh around his eyes and mouth seemed loose, doughy. When he spoke, he slurred. "The honorable thing."

"I'm trying to save them, and you're making it impossible." Picard walked toward him.

"It *is* impossible."

A frightened Romulan and a drunk Klingon. "You seem to be agreeing with T'sart," Picard said.

Kalor coughed, what might have been his weak attempt at a chuckle. "Then he is not always a fool."

"Or you both are."

The Klingon shook his head. "You have a mission. Complete it."

"I can do that *and* save those ships," Picard said.

"I disagree. They're my ships. I will do what . . . what I see fit."

Picard nodded and leaned down over the desk. "And this is my ship. And I'll do as I see fit. I'm saving those vessels. You can make that easier for me, or more difficult. But I'll do it, without or without your help." He swiveled the computer around toward Kalor. "Call them. Now."

"Status, Spock." Picard marched onto the bridge.

"The Klingons are maneuvering back this way, as quickly as they can."

Picard nodded.

"They'll need to transfer all their battery power to their structural integrity fields," Spock said.

Kalor nodded as he came out of Picard's office, suppressing an obvious stagger. "I have alerted them."

"Helm," Picard said, "plot a course into the dead zone. We'll lose power and maneuverability quickly. Stand by on tractor beams." He turned to Spock. "You're sure this will keep the Klingon ships from careening out of control?"

"Negative. Once in the dead zone, we may not have the power to tractor seven separate vessels all being pushed at near light speed."

With so many people lost on the planet . . . well, Picard wanted to save those he could, now that he wasn't optionless. He looked up toward the Klingon governor, who was leaning across the upper bridge handrail, supporting his bulk clumsily and without much dignity. "We'll save whom we can."

Kalor nodded. "I know."

Enterprise Runabout *Kaku*
Romulan space
Sector 18

"I'd like to trust you . . ." Riker sighed and looked away from Tobin's sad, almost childlike face. He felt as if he was having to tell a little boy he'd just accidentally killed his pet puppy.

"I would . . . like you to trust me," Tobin said, and seemed to be attempting a hopeful smile. He reclined in one of the runabout chairs, and so looked even more disarmed than his smile alone painted him.

Riker looked up at Deanna and she didn't give him the encouraging nod he was hoping for. He looked back to Tobin. "We have a mission," he tried to explain. "It's very important. I can't take the chance that our meeting you isn't a coincidence."

Lowering his head with a slow nod, Tobin seemed to be considering that. "I do not know what I could say to prove to you my honesty and sincerity."

What Riker probably couldn't explain, so he didn't want to try, was that there was nothing Tobin *could* say.

There was just too much at risk to invest even more time in this man and his ship. The problem was, they couldn't just leave him to go on his way, either.

"Tobin," Riker began. "It's not just a matter of your not being able to come with us . . ."

The Romulan looked up, from Riker to Data, then to Deanna and back to Riker. "You are going to kill me?"

"Of course not!" Deanna said.

"No, no." Riker ran his hand through his hair. "But I am going to have Mr. Data disable your vessel."

"You . . . why?" The Romulan's brows knitted together in confusion.

"Because . . ." How could Riker explain this? "Look, it will only be enough to keep you here for a few days. Life support will be fine. Your cloak will be fine. But you won't be able to maneuver or use communications. You'll be able to repair the systems you need, but probably won't finish until we're out of Romulan space."

Tobin frowned. He wasn't a moron. He understood. He was just incredulous. "You're going to intentionally damage my vessel."

"I . . . I'm sorry, Mr. Tobin." Riker looked at Deanna again. She was the empath, but he knew she felt sorry for him.

"I suppose I understand." The Romulan said slowly. "I have . . . perhaps strangely, enjoyed this encounter, nevertheless."

One thing was certain, Tobin knew how to lay on the guilt.

Romulan Warbird *Makluan*
Klingon/Romulan border
Sector 5

"Why?" Folan kept asking herself. Why would T'sart defect to the Federation? What reason could take him from his relatively high degree of prestige and power?

She'd been acting on anger until now and not using her best asset—her intellect. T'sart had always used his mind to his advantage. Folan had to do the same.

If she could know *what* he and Picard were doing, she might also figure out the why and the how. Then she would know what she had to do to stop them.

She bounded from the command chair and up to Medric's station. "How complete was T'sart's deletion of his files from our databanks?"

Medric stared at her blankly for a moment, then finally said, "I don't know. I've not looked."

Folan felt a tightness in her chest. "Then *look.*" It didn't seem that Medric was going to make any of this easy for her.

He glowered at his computer screen a few long moments as she stood waiting. "Personal files are gone," he said. "Wiped. Not even fragments left. But we still have logs of computer usage. Those can't be erased."

Folan was almost surprised T'sart hadn't figured out a way. "If we look at these, what might they tell us?"

"They won't tell you anything," Medric said, and she noted he'd said "you" and not "us."

"They wouldn't exist if they didn't tell us something."

"Fine. They won't tell you *much:* Periods of computer use. Databases accessed. Files open, closed, saved, deleted . . . standard actions."

Folan nodded, her mind already churning on the possibilities. "Transfer those logs to this station." She pointed at her old station. She was careful not to refer to it that way, though. "I want to see them all."

"Fine." Medric tapped the appropriate keys on his console.

The tension was thick. Folan hated it, but would endure. She must. She'd started this and swore she'd see it to its end.

She slid into the science station seat and began poring over the download. At first the logs were just a jumble of dates and times, filenames and deletions. She couldn't make much of it. How could she hunt an animal that floated above the ground and left no tracks? Folan was no hunter.

But she *was* a scientist. She could look for a pattern. Any pattern.

First dates, then common file names. Then databases he used. And reused. And what sort of information each database held.

After more than an hour she raised her head from the console. "I have something," she said, her throat dry.

No one paid her any mind.

"Medric," she said in a commanding tone, "come here."

He rose, stepped over, and stood at her side. "Yes, Sub-Commander," he said, his tone bland.

She pointed toward one of the monitors. "Look."

He leaned down. "What am I supposed to see?"

Folan wanted to hit him, like she had her younger brothers when they'd annoyed her beyond imagination. "On three separate occasions, T'sart requested patrol information for sectors 18 through 50."

Medric grunted. "He's been nowhere near that sector. And we weren't going to be."

She nodded somewhat excitedly. "Exactly."

"So?" He shrugged. "There's nothing in that area anyway. A few outward colonies. Nothing important. It's too far out."

"Yes. But T'sart was interested."

He breathed out through his nose and leaned down closer to the console, this time with intent. "He wants something out there, or wanted to travel out that way."

Folan nodded. "Yes. The question is 'what'?" She tapped at her board and a list of files flashed on another screen. "The only thing of even mild interest in this area is a subspace relay station."

"Only he would know," Medric said, but his tone was much less bored now.

"That's not all I've found. Our sensor logs show a subspace burst from the *Enterprise* when they were still in Romulan space. Here, look." She pointed to yet another monitor graphing a list of sensor anomalies. "A warp vessel," she said. "A small one."

"Perhaps," Medric was suddenly slower to agree, "were we able to alert the fleet—"

"We're not." Folan snapped.

"So, what does this do for us?" Medric asked.

"I'm not sure of that part," she admitted. "But the

only thing I can see of importance in this area is a relay hub that processes communications and computer database updates throughout these sectors. At first, I thought perhaps he needed some information from it."

"What kind of information?"

"No, listen, I rethought that. Relay stations like that are also used for emergency supply stores. There's an element they might be looking for there. They could add it to their warp intermix or plasma conduits and mask their warp signature to look like that of a warbird's."

Medric shook his head and frowned deeply. "That is not possible."

"It is," Folan corrected him. "I submitted a report to the Senate two years ago on this, but it was ignored. My specialty is power and energy systems, remember?"

Nodding slowly, Medric rubbed his forehead thoughtfully and leaned slightly on the lip of the science station. "Then why are T'sart and the *Enterprise* now in Klingon space?"

"I wondered that, too. I think it's to throw us off. And I have a way to throw *them* off." Folan felt a chuckle rise in her chest. "We're still getting computer database updates from that relay station. All we need do is send some information back."

"What kind of information? The station is unmanned."

Folan stood. "That's why this works. We can extrapolate, from when the *Enterprise* shuttle left, an approximate time they're likely to arrive at the relay hub. If we pinpoint it correctly, they'll be docked when we've timed the station to self-destruct."

"Send it a command to self-destruct," Medric repeated. "That is . . . interesting."

"Is that almost a compliment, Centurion?"

He was quiet for a moment, then finally mumbled, "Almost."

Folan smiled. "Call up the access codes and schematics of that relay station."

He nodded. "Right away."

U.S.S. Enterprise, NCC 1701-E
Klingon space
Malinga Sector

"Ten seconds," Spock called from the science station, his voice calm but not quite monotone.

Picard nodded. He wondered if this was how Kirk had felt, working with the Vulcan. Complete trust flowed between them. "Ready on tractor beams, Mr. Chamberlain."

"Ready, sir."

The captain lowered himself into the command chair. "Batten down, everyone."

"My ships are ready," Kalor said as he took a seat next to Picard. "They are transferring power to inertial dampers, even from life support."

"Five seconds."

Picard looked back toward Spock, then forward toward the main viewer as the Vulcan continued the countdown.

"Engage!"

"Three . . ."

A small flash point of light at the center of the forward viewer. *Enterprise* sped toward it, then slowed abnormally as she hit the edge of the dead zone.

"Two . . ."

The flash bubbled out, then dissipated. On the viewscreen, Picard saw the Klingon ships gathered together.

"One . . ."

Space was silent, but Picard could imagine the rumble. Just now they were seeing the matter/antimatter explosions that had occurred four hours before.

"Tractor beams! Now!"

"Shockwave!" Spock called.

A rush of spatial disruption pushed out in all directions. *Enterprise*'s thrusters whined to keep her slowed and controlled as the Klingon ships pitched backward with the blast, tumbling end over end. Seven thin lines of energy connected them with *Enterprise*, lashing them together to keep them from bounding out into space without direction.

Picard's ship bonded herself to them, and as they were bulldozed away, *Enterprise* was dragged with them, tumbling.

Chapter Twenty-one

Enterprise *runabout* Kaku
Romulan space
Sector 35

"DID YOU SEE THE LOOK ON HIS FACE?" Deanna tapped at the console before her. There wasn't much to do, but she kept pulling up different sections of the sector to scan.

"I saw the look," Riker admitted.

She frowned, but knew he couldn't see it. "All things considered, he took it very well."

"You would know."

"I'm sorry?" She swiveled toward him and a long thread of her black hair bounced before her eyes. She pushed it away. "I'm an empath, not a mind-reader. I can't know when someone's lying."

"What did I say?" He met her eyes, then returned to

the safety of his navi-console. "I wasn't blaming you for not being able to read his mind."

"Yes, you were. I *can* read *your* mind." Deanna felt his frustration, and it compounded her own.

"I just don't see what good it does to tell me he's disappointed in us," Riker grumbled.

"I wasn't telling you for a reason. I was telling you because that's what he felt."

"Well," Riker slapped at his controls harder than need be. "He should keep his feelings to himself."

"He was," Deanna said.

"Then *you* should keep his feelings to himself."

A wave of his anger scraped across her. "I think you're being overly hostile because you're not at all sure it was necessary to disable the poor man's ship."

"Now he's a poor man?" Riker asked exasperatedly.

"Yes."

"Look, Deanna, I'm *not* sure it was all that necessary to do what we did. But it *was* prudent. We don't know this guy, you can't read his mind—"

"See? Hostility."

Riker sighed. "What else should I have done?"

She thought about that a moment, and when she answered, she made sure her voice was softer. "I don't know, Will. I'm sorry. Of course it was wise, I'm sure. I just feel sorry for him."

"If we fail, he won't be around to be felt sorry for."

She nodded. "True."

Data spoke, reminding Deanna he was at the rear scanning station. "May I interrupt your argument?"

She smiled. "We're not arguing, Data."

"We're discussing," Riker said.

"With him in a testy mood."

"I am *not* testy."

Deanna rolled her eyes.

Data said, "We will be approaching the relay station soon."

"Any vessels in this sector?" Riker turned to his own scanners.

"None, sir."

"Increase power to the sensors by seventy percent. I'd like a better long-range look."

The android nodded. "Aye, sir. However, that will burn out the sensor circuits in less than twelve hours."

"We have to rendezvous with the *Enterprise* in 15 hours. Think you can stretch it?"

"I will try, sir."

"Thank you, Data." Riker smiled, but Deanna felt no change in his mood.

"He is not testy with me," Data whispered to Deanna as he turned away.

"Faker," she mumbled.

Romulan Warbird *Makluan*
Klingon space
Malinga sector

"Are you ready?" Folan was rather excited. This was the first time since command had fallen on her that she felt perhaps she need not fight to keep it. "How long will it take to send?"

"I am ready," Medric said, and though she searched his tone she could not find much hostility. "Thankfully, the transmission doesn't require the main subspace communications array."

Folan didn't chuckle, but she let her voice be a bit lighter, and she decided not to pursue the obvious reminder that they didn't have audio or visual subspace communications. "My question remains unanswered."

He continued tapping at his controls and didn't look up. "From this distance, it will be a few minutes after we initiate the program code."

"And it will destroy the relay complex?"

"And any vessel within a twenty-thousand kilometer radius."

Pleased, she nodded. "Good. Good." She'd been grasping at straws, struggling with decisions she wouldn't truly know the outcome of. Until now. This felt concrete. This felt right.

Medric turned to her. "Have you considered that our calculations of when the *Enterprise*'s shuttle will arrive at the relay might be incorrect?"

Even Medric couldn't stifle her good feeling. "There hasn't been time for them to arrive yet. Of that I'm sure. Even traveling at their top speed, at the route they'll need to take to avoid detection . . ."

"And if they should arrive after the relay station has self-destructed?" He was trying to ruin it, wasn't he?

"Answer your own question by answering this," Folan said. "What will happen when a subspace relay station suddenly stops working, and long-range sensor scans indicate it was destroyed?"

He huffed out a short breath. "It will be investigated. Expeditiously."

She leaned down close to him and almost whispered. "By whom?"

"At the very least, a warbird will be dispatched."

"At the *very* least," Folan said, rolling the thought around her head and the words around her tongue. "And probably more than that."

Medric nodded, satisfied.

Folan smiled. "They're as good as dead. Now we just have to deal with Picard and T'sart themselves."

U.S.S. Enterprise, NCC 1701-E
Klingon Empire
Malinga Sector

"Thirty degrees pitch!" Rossi cried.

"Stabilizers!" Picard ordered as he white-knuckled the arms of the command chair.

"Trying, sir."

"We're losing power." Spock's voice.

The captain heard La Forge on the comm. *"Inertial dampers down by fourteen percent."*

Picard glanced at a status screen to his right. "Aux power!"

"Transferring."

The vessel shook around them, the bridge shuddering seemingly to its rivets. Picard felt it in his bones, in his teeth. "Tractor status!"

"Maintaining," Chamberlain said with a grunt as the ship bounced under them. "Barely."

"Spock, how much—" And suddenly, it stopped. "—longer?" Silence. Like waking from a nightmare.

"I believe it is over, Captain." Spock said dryly.

Pulling in a long breath, Picard rose, straightening his tunic. "Status."

"Warp power was off-line due to a plasma injector imbalance. Mr. La Forge reports that has been solved. Minor injuries, minor damage."

"Klingons' status?"

Spock tapped at the science station scanners. "Four of the seven Klingon vessels are intact."

Kalor staggered forward. "Parl . . ."

"Your personal vessel has survived," Spock told him, "but is severely damaged."

The Klingon looked toward the forward veiwscreen, though it showed nothing. "How damaged?"

"Three of the four have at least auxiliary power. They all have life support. No hull breaches."

"Three ships gone. Three. And an entire planet. Nineteen million people," Kalor said slowly. "My people. Under my charge."

If only that were the end of it, Picard thought. On that planet was the data on T'sart's virus. If he died now, without explaining all he knew about the dead zones . . . this was the fate of every technologically civilized planet. Including Earth.

Chapter Twenty-two

Enterprise runabout *Kaku*
Romulan space
Sector 36

"IT IS EERILY QUIET." Deanna looked out the forward port at the small relay station. It wasn't in a star system, but just hanging out in space, illuminated only by its own running lights.

"That's good," Riker said. "No one's supposed to be here."

She continued to gaze at the station's rather graceful arms. Shaped like a giant flower, each petal had what looked like a deflector array at its end. It was peaceful. Beautiful, in fact. "For some reason, when invading enemy space I think of conflict more than serenity."

"We could argue again if you'd like," Riker offered, along with a playful smile.

Deanna returned the smile. "I thought we were only discussing."

"That, too." He twisted a half turn toward aft. "Anything new on those enhanced long-range sensors, Data?"

"Nothing, sir. Still reading the two warbirds. One in orbit around a planet in the Galaras system, the other heading toward the Romulan homeworld."

Deanna noticed how, even with his emotion chip enabled, Data's voice remained mostly unchanged. A slight difference, she supposed, but most people would probably not notice.

"Current distance?" Riker asked.

"Three parsecs and seven point nine parsecs respectively, sir."

Riker frowned and, as usual, Deanna felt his change in emotion flow over her. In a way, it was like listening to an orchestra. Sometimes one set of instruments could be heard over the others. Now she "heard" a sense of caution.

"Three parsecs is a little closer than I'd like," he said. "They could scan us."

"I am modulating our warp signature to resemble that of a Romulan shuttle," Data said.

"Good. See if you can pull up any info on one of their shuttles. Might be good if we matched their plasma emissions and other characteristics they might be able to scan."

"Aye, sir." Data liked the idea and sounded cheerful. "Perhaps I could—"

An audio alarm rang and brought all their attention forward.

In front of them, the relay station flashed brightly and then ruptured outward with a white-hot glow.

"What the hell—" Riker spun toward the side console. "Shields!"

Chunks of molten debris slammed into the quickly raised deflectors, bouncing the runabout as she turned away.

"Inertial dampers failing," Data called.

Riker struggled with the helm. Deanna caught glances of him as he grunted to hold a course. She was bounced out of her chair and onto the deck. The lip of her seat caught her neck and the lights dimmed, or her consciousness did. She wasn't sure which.

"Hold on!" Riker's voice. It sounded faint. She tried to pull herself up, but darkness swirled around her and she fell into it.

"How long?" Riker's head felt as if it weighed a hundred kilos and his voice sounded shallow, but he struggled his way mostly upright, leaning on the bulkhead. "How long?" He asked again.

"You have both been unconscious for three minutes, nineteen seconds," Data said.

Both. Riker turned to one side, then the other, before he saw Deanna to his left. "Deanna?"

She groaned and her head shifted as she lay face-up on the deck.

"I scanned you both briefly with a medical tricorder," Data said as Riker tilted her up softly. "No serious injuries, though you'd both succumbed to stray coolant fumes. And Counselor Troi has a bruise on her left cheek."

Riker looked down and checked each side of her ivory face. "I don't see one."

Data looked back a moment, then toward the forward port. "Not *that* left cheek, sir."

Figuring that information was received from the tricorder, Riker saw Deanna's eye fluttering open and he helped her up. "Are you okay?"

"I seem to have fallen," she said, sliding back into her chair.

"Me, too." Riker gripped the back of her seat. He was still a bit off balance himself.

"You okay?" she asked.

"Yes." He tapped Data on the shoulder and Data let Riker take the helm chair. "Status?"

The android slid into the scanning station next to Deanna. "Debris from the relay station explosion damaged one of our warp nacelle stabilizers, and main inertial dampers were knocked off-line. I have compensated with backup systems, but our maximum speed is reduced, and we have a small plasma leak."

"How small?"

Data nodded. He obviously understood Riker's concern. "Big enough for them to see, sir."

And it didn't take long. A Romulan warbird, the one that had been closest, was on an intercept course.

"I don't suppose evasive maneuvers are called for." Deanna touched Riker's shoulder supportively.

Riker suppressed a sigh. "I'm not sure what good it'd do."

"They will intercept us in three minutes, seventeen seconds," Data reported.

A little over three minutes. The runabout was no match for a warbird. They were outclassed in size, speed, and—since they were damaged—maneuverability. "Options?" Riker might as well ask, since he couldn't think of any.

After he thought a moment, Data answered. "None that I am aware of, sir."

Suddenly Riker remembered something. "Are they cloaked?"

"Yes, sir."

"So they don't know we see them?"

Data considered that briefly. "I think we can surmise that."

"Okay, that's good. We can use that."

"How?" Deanna asked.

The plan wasn't all clear in his mind quite yet, but Riker knew if he talked it out, the idea would formulate. "The longer they're just watching us before attacking, the longer we can travel without interference, right?"

"We can't make it all the way to the rendezvous point," Deanna said. "We'd be too early anyway."

"Don't need to make it all the way there. Just a few more minutes," Riker said, and he now knew what they needed to do. He looked at his scanner monitor.

"Sir, the warbird is decloaking," Data said. "They are within torpedo range."

Riker looked up. *Damn,* he thought. *They came in too fast.* "Communications?"

"Jammed, sir."

"Great," Riker grumbled. "Data, can you still scan Mr. Tobin's ship?"

"No, sir. We left it cloaked." The android checked his scanners again. "I cannot verify it is there, but we did disable its propulsion. Our previous coordinates should be correct."

"But if it's drifted . . . Damn, I wish we could contact him."

Riker felt Deanna's hand on his shoulder again. "Will, if you involve him in this and something goes wrong—"

He shook his head. "Everything is pretty wrong now, Deanna. We don't have many choices."

"The Romulans are attempting a tractor beam," Data said. "The plasma leak is hampering their effort."

"Good. Do we have phasers?"

"Aye, sir."

"See if you can't disable a few of their tractor generators," Riker ordered.

Data nodded and tapped at his controls. The runabout whined as she lanced phasers into the large warbird's shields. But one bee won't bring down a gorilla. It was a futile ploy, Riker knew.

The Romulans lashed back with disruptors. Weapons fire crackled over the runabout's weak shields and jostled everyone aboard.

"Shields down seventy-three percent," Deanna said. "Warp engines are off-line."

Riker grunted. He was a fair pilot, but with one nacelle venting plasma, warp power off-line, and only backup dampers working . . . "We have to do this now, before we lose the power."

"I have the coordinates of Tobin's vessel," Data said.

"Within range?" Riker noticed his tone was tense. Only Data and Deanna around, he didn't really need to cover his emotions. Deanna felt them anyway.

"At extreme range in twelve seconds."

"If he hasn't moved. If he has, we'll beam into open space."

"Isn't transporting a little risky at this speed?" Deanna asked, most of her concentration on the power graphs.

Her question went unanswered. Their vessel shook harshly as the warbird's weapons bashed against dying shields and buckling hull plates.

"No other choice," Riker said. "Range?"

"Four seconds."

Riker clicked off the ticks in his head, then . . .

"Data, now!"

Chapter Twenty-three

Private Bird-of-Prey, Klingon design
Klingon Empire
Lormit Sector

"YOU'RE INSANE." Gorlat neither smiled nor hissed. He was matter-of-fact and completely blunt. "That's all. You've just lost your tiny, warped Klingon brain."

Lotre remained silent and continued packing gear into one of the locker compartments.

"I must agree," said the Andorian in his raspy whisper.

"Topor, you'd agree with the animal who killed your mother," one of the other mercenaries said. Lotre didn't see who.

"My own father killed my mother," Topor purred.

"And you agreed with him," Gorlat said.

Topor smiled thinly and shrugged. "I hired him. What is your point?"

Lotre sighed. "While my ancestry may be Klingon, my brain is Romulan—"

"Is that supposed to be better?" scoffed one of the nine different aliens gathered about.

"Yes," Lotre said. "It is."

"Ravings," someone said. "We're asking for death," another complained. And again, Gorlat said, "You're crazy, Lotre."

"I am not insane."

"Then you're drugged." Gorlat pushed Lotre away from the lockers, as if Lotre wasn't done and on his way anyway.

"I am not drugged."

"Insane or drugged, *I* care not. We'll all be just as dead if we continue to follow this ship."

Lotre noticed that while Gorlat spoke for himself and probably most of the others, they were all stowing their gear nonetheless. "You're supposed to be mercenaries. You're paid to do as you're told."

"I'm paid to fight," Gorlat said. "Not to die."

Lotre smiled. "Fight *well,* and you won't die."

"Against a starship? *That* starship? In case you'd not noticed, *that* is the *Enterprise.*"

"I noticed. We'll have help, from the inside." Lotre turned to them, and smiled. "Now what do you say?"

Gorlat sneered. "I say the help'd better be flippin' divine."

U.S.S. Enterprise, NCC 1701-E
Klingon Empire
Lormit Sector

"Captain, we're reading increased neutrino emissions." Spock had been at the science station, waiting for just such an occurrence.

"They're closing in," Picard said, stepping up toward the Vulcan.

Spock turned toward the captain. "A logical assumption." He had that glint in his eye. Smiling, without actually smiling.

"Within transporter range?" Picard asked.

"In . . . seventeen seconds," Spock answered with just a slight glance at the console.

Picard turned toward tactical. "Mr. Chamberlain, silent signal of general quarters and intruder alert. Notify Mr. La Forge."

"Aye, sir."

Determined, the captain turned back, his jaw tight.

"Stand by, Mr. Sp—"

Cut off by a low rumble and then an alert, Picard stopped instantly and listened. Somewhere, deep within the ship, a series of explosions vibrated up to the bridge.

"Captain," Chamberlain called, "shields are down! We've lost the main shield conduits."

"Reroute, Ensign! And now, Mr. Spock. Now!"

The whole process lasted longer than it should have, and for a very brief moment he thought he might actually panic. It was a common phobia, but he pushed it away. He knew that when he finally did materialize, there would be much to do.

Lotre experienced the final stage of transport when his feeling slowly returned. His skin tingled and then his sight was restored in a hail of harsh sparkle. *Enterprise*'s engineering room appeared before him. His disruptor already raised, Lotre targeted the nearest Starfleeter and fired.

The man crumpled, stunned into submission. Lotre targeted another, by his rank probably the chief engineer, but the dark man jumped behind a console. "Fan out," Lotre ordered, and gave chase.

The engineer was fast and well trained. He rolled away quickly, and when he came up on a knee, Lotre assumed he'd have a weapon. He did. The mercenary bowed left and protected himself behind a support strut. He glanced back at the nine others who had beamed in with him. They were all still standing, but only two of the Starfleeters were yet down. Two down, hundreds to go? Only if Lotre couldn't get to environmental control and the bridge.

"Secure engineering," Lotre ordered, "I will proceed with the plan and meet the othe—"

Squinting in sudden pain, Lotre pressed his free hand's fingers into his skull above one ear. "Sonic!" he grunted.

"They don't hear it," cried one of his men. "Earplugs."

Something Lotre hadn't thought to bring. "Find where it's coming from!"

A painful distraction that could win this battle for the Starfleeters. Lotre looked for any speaker centers or communications hubs, and at the same time needed to defend himself from phaser shots. He darted between support struts, painfully zeroing in on the place from where the sonic whine seemed to emanate.

He reached for his tricorder, but the scanning device was missing. Odd—he'd not felt it drop. Too small a concern to occupy his mind now. The pain in his head was too great. He felt the sound reverberate throughout his skull, now his spine and breastbone. He couldn't take anymore. He fired toward the area wildly. Foolish, really—his own orders were to maintain stun settings so that neither necessary equipment nor necessary personnel would be damaged.

Disruptor energy punched forward from his weapon and slammed into a force field. Containment fields! "They had time to raise containment fields!" Lotre screamed in pain, but fought to keep himself from grumbling. He reset his rifle to full and fired a prolonged burst.

Raw energy finally pushed past the electronic barrier and the console exploded. Fire suppression force fields quickly surrounded the flames, but smoke had already plumed into the room.

Lotre coughed hard, but the painful noise was gone and he ran toward the exit. The air was cleaner in the corridor, and he remembered the deck map clearly as he turned toward the turbolift, and the armory.

"Two sets of ten life-forms have transported aboard, sir." Chamberlain's voice was thick with apprehension. He anxiously leaned on one leg and then the other as he stood at the tactical station. "Shields are still down."

"La Forge?" Picard asked.

Chamberlain shook his head. "Comm systems are down, too. Also due to internal explosions."

"Sabotage," Picard growled. "Ensign Bradley." The captain motioned the man quickly forward. "Alert security. I want the guard doubled around T'sart."

"Aye, sir."

"Chalna, find La Forge and get him to find a way to bypass the destroyed conduits. Sanderson, I want status from every deck. You'll have to go on foot."

All three cleared out for the turbolifts.

The captain pivoted toward the upper deck. "Mr. Spock?"

Spock nodded but didn't look up from his internal ship's scanners. "Internal sensors show all intruders are accounted for. One of the ten from Engineering is on his way to deck twelve." He looked up and met Picard's eyes. "Engineering has been secured by the intruders."

"They've been lucky until now," the captain said. "Let's see that luck doesn't hold."

Spock's left hand glided over his console. "Aye, sir."

Lotre stopped quickly, catching himself before he entered the turbolift. Obviously the sonics had left him more disoriented than he thought. He knew better than to confine himself in an elevator, and he'd committed to memory every ladder access he'd need and a few he shouldn't, but might. And he'd wasted time running in the opposite direction.

Dull footsteps echoed up the corridor. *Damn Federation! What kind of warship has carpeted halls?* Boots on metal would have alerted Lotre sooner; now he had only seconds.

Ducking into a doorway alcove, Lotre hid and waited until he could hear their breathing. He quietly reset his weapon to wide stun, and when he heard them close enough, he curled his weapon arm into the hall and fired.

Lotre fell to one knee and rolled across the corridor and into the next alcove. He was one of twenty men on a ship full of Federation soldiers. He would take no chances.

When he glanced up the hall during his roll, he saw all four security officers were down, stunned. He sighed, rolled back into the corridor, and jumped into a run. Leaping over the Starfleeters, Lotre fired up the hall as two more rounded a corner. They quickly deflated and collapsed to the deck.

He couldn't help but smile. It was going well. Very well. And then, suddenly, it wasn't.

A force field snapped to life and blocked his way.

Anger furrowed his brows where nature had not, and he pushed against the field for a frustrating moment. A foolish and yet instinctive reaction to being trapped— test the cage.

A waste of time, he thought, and knew he didn't have the time to squander. To snare him, they'd had to have known where to find him. He probably had only seconds.

He pulled a small device from a pouch in his tunic and set it on the deck. A one-use force-field disruption unit. He'd thought he'd need to use it around the bridge or the armory, but he needed it now for the force fields that ran through the ship's bulkheads and decks. Resetting his disruptor, he aimed it at the floor and pulled the rifle's trigger. A cascade of sound and energy squashed the deck beneath it. Spark and smoke gushed toward his head and he bowed away, but continued to fire. First just burning, then melting, the floor finally gave way and crashed to the deck below.

Lotre leapt and followed it down, his boots crunching into molten debris as he landed roughly and nearly stumbled. He jumped again, this time off the rubble he'd created and onto the clean floor.

The corridor was clear, but above him he heard the cursing of those looking for him in their trap.

Now he had to run—they would be on him again, and soon.

Two decks away he'd find reinforcements. His men were in the main armory, beamed directly there, and that would be where most of the *Enterprise* security personnel would be. There, and trying to get his other nine mercenaries out of Engineering.

"Status?" Picard asked Chamberlain.

"Commander La Forge is working on the shields, sir. No ETA yet. I have a weapons lock on the enemy ship. They've scanned us, so they know it. They're just waiting."

"Waiting for their boarding party to get a foothold. We can't accommodate that many more. We need those shields up." Picard paced toward tactical and looked over Chamberlain's shoulder. "Just in case, arm the crew. Hand phasers for all personnel."

"Aye, sir."

Spock approached and handed Picard a sidearm. He also holstered one for himself.

"I want to know *how* we were damaged. And by whom," Picard said as he took the weapon.

"I shall investigate," Spock said. "The enemy number in Engineering is down to six. They've sealed themselves in and are attempting to override environmental and helm controls."

The captain pursed his lips and marched back toward the command chair. "Make it difficult for them."

"Of course," Spock said.

"What about the other team?"

"The armory." The Vulcan turned toward one of the sensor readouts on the console behind him. He tapped at the controls. "Ten life-forms of various races, with one of the enemy force from Engineering apparently making his way there. A Klingon."

"Interesting," Picard said. "A Klingon working for a Romulan?"

"Not unheard of."

"Indeed not. Just unusual."

"The question is, why would he break away from those he beamed in with?"

"Easy answer." Picard stood and walked toward Spock. "He's in charge." He leaned over Spock's shoulder and watched the sensor readouts. "His people secured Engineering, and now he'll make sure they secure the armory."

Spock nodded. "Very logical, Captain."

"I have my moments," Picard said. "Let's see that

their leader gets a leader's welcome outside the armory. Add a few more to the security team."

Spock's fingers did a lithe dance on the computer console. "Added."

"We'll see how long it takes him to get into the armory now."

"Hold it right there, Mister."

Lotre turned quickly and ducked into a doorway alcove for cover.

He got a quick glimpse of the officer who'd caught him short. Red accents and the rank of commander, if he wasn't mistaken. Looked like the first officer, Riker.

The tall Starfleeter had just a hand phaser, but he seemed to know how to use it. Lotre was pinned down, and if he allowed that for much longer there would be a swarm of security officers around him.

So damn close to the armory, he thought. A phaser shot sizzled past his head and was absorbed into the bulkhead close to him. Heavy stun. Federation fools. If his ship was the one being invaded, he'd be firing to kill.

"It's over," Riker said. "Give it up."

Starfleet arrogance at work. Lotre was nowhere near ready to give anything up. He had a few stun grenades, but the problem with those was that they were really more for a covert operation. Tossing a stun grenade at someone who saw it coming and could disable it with a well-placed phaser shot . . . well, it wouldn't do too much good. But as a distraction . . .

He took one grenade, then decided to take another as

well. He punched in the codes to arm them and tossed them up the hall toward the Starfleeter.

Jumping forward as the grenades clattered up the deck, Lotre rolled along the floor and around the corner. He heard Riker fire twice to disable the grenades. As he assumed the Starfleeter would.

He peeked up the corridor and saw no one coming from in front of him. But when he turned quickly back around—

"Drop it." Riker was standing there, close enough to have his phaser aimed right at him, point-blank, but far enough away to be out of easy striking range.

"How—" Lotre was amazed.

Riker stepped forward and kicked the Klingon's rifle up the hallway. It skittered against the deck and out of reach. Lotre looked from Riker to his weapon, then back to Riker. He rose slowly, feigning a defeated posture.

Gesturing for him to take a walk up the corridor, Riker was sure to keep his distance. All that meant to Lotre was that he'd have to lunge.

He landed painfully on his elbows at Riker's feet, and managed to pull the Starfleeter's legs out from under him. Riker fell back with a grunt and Lotre pulled the man's tall frame toward him. As Riker struggled to rise without leverage, Lotre grappled for the phaser.

The Starfleeter's grip was like iron and Lotre grumbled, "How strong are you?"

Smiling, Riker said, "Stronger than you," and he kicked out from underneath the Klingon, sending him a few feet down the corridor.

His right leg taking most of the blow as he fell on the

deck, Lotre got up quickly. He didn't have the phaser, but somehow neither did Riker. Lotre saw it, leapt for it, and rolled shoulder to knee as he grabbed it.

Now Riker was the captive, Lotre thought, and smiled.

Oddly, Riker was smiling, too. Startled for a moment by the expression, Lotre hesitated at the blur that Riker became, gray and red suddenly close to him.

"By the Praetor—" Lotre gasped, and Riker was right there, backhanding him onto the deck.

Rage boiled deep without the Klingon. When he spoke he was sputtering with fury. "How the devil are you so strong?"

Riker scooped up Lotre's disruptor rifle and leveled it at him.

For a short moment Lotre actually felt defeated, his head pounding in anger. But the warm Federation phaser was still in his hand. He didn't look down at it, but his thumb found the setting control and leaned heavily on it. He fired, and a thin but powerful orange thread connected Riker with the weapon.

Riker howled as the beam swiped down into his weapon arm. Sizzling through flesh and bone, sealing the wound with the same heat that cut it, the rifle— with Riker's arm still attached—fell to the deck.

The Starfleeter collapsed in agony and rolled into the bulkhead.

Lotre scooped up the disruptor rifle. The Klingon checked the weapon's power cell and available state, and chucked it into ready position.

Gorlat approached from up the corridor, various scattered bodies, the stunned carcasses of Starfleet security, littering his path.

He kicked one, for good measure and probably for personal pleasure.

"It is done," he said.

Lotre looked down at Riker's shocky, quivering form and smirked. "So is he."

"Having a central armory is insane," Gorlat snorted. "We vaporized their store in a matter of minutes."

Lotre moved to the next nearest Starfleeter and took his weapon. "But you saved the power packs, correct? We can convert them for our own weapons."

"Of course. This is *not* my first such mission."

"It is your first Federation Battle Cruiser," Lotre said, taking the next man's weapon, too, and handing it to his comrade.

Gorlat couldn't seem to argue with what Lotre said, so he merely grunted.

"It's time to bring the others." Lotre pulled out a communicator and brought it to his lips. "This is Lotre. Teams three through five, begin transport."

Static crackled back at him and a small spike of apprehension raised the hairs on the back of his neck.

"Topor! Respond!"

Again, biting silence.

"Topor? Lormit? Anyone, respond!"

Nothing.

"We're being jammed, or they've been silenced at the source."

Gorlat snarled. "We cannot maintain control of this vessel with so few men. We were supposed to be the advance team to make sure they couldn't get their shields back up, and to take out their armory without destroying the rest of the ship."

Marching up the corridor, Lotre spat, "I know the plan, Gorlat! It was a strategy of my own creation!"

"What do we do now?"

"Gather your team," the Klingon said. "We take the bridge, and find out what has happened to our ship."

"The bridge will be heavily protected."

"And we," Lotre said indignantly, "will be heavily armed."

The Starfleeters were formidable, there was no denying that. They'd cut off the turbolifts, and when Lotre found a transporter room, that proved to be useless, too. This was not how it was supposed to have been.

The plan had been to secure Engineering and the armory, assuring the shields would stay down and the crew would not be armed. Then Lotre would have been free to beam a team directly onto the bridge.

Now he had no such support.

"Three of you take that hatchway," Lotre ordered. "The rest of you, with me."

He didn't like breaking up such a small number, but with the lifts not working that meant more than no one could easily get on the bridge; it meant no one could easily get off.

The three would attempt access through the conduits that serviced the exterior of the bridge. Lotre would take the rest via an open lift shaft.

Without help, he pried the turbolift doors open.

"Hold them," he ordered whoever reached out first. Gorlat held them open as Lotre pulled a small device from a pocket and stuck it inside the lift shaft. He switched the small apparatus on.

"Someone check that."

One of the others pulled out a small scanner unit and nodded. "Sensor dampener functional."

Lotre ducked his head in and twisted his gaze upward. "Fools didn't lock the car at the top. We have access."

"It could be booby-trapped."

The Klingon nodded. "Yes, Gorlat, it could. You go first."

Gorlat sneered, but leapt to the tube's hand-rungs and began climbing.

The ascent was tedious and, for Lotre, angst-ridden. He tried only to focus on each rung as he rose hand over hand, but his mind kept whirling around the possibilities. He could not hold captive hundreds of Starfleet crew with twenty men. It was going to be difficult with two hundred. And if they couldn't communicate with their reinforcements . . .

By the time they'd reached the top, it was obvious there was no defense perimeter, no booby-traps.

Gorlat stood off on a narrow slice of ledge to one side of the closed entry. He reached to open the door with his hands, but Lotre motioned him off. "Too slow," he mouthed quietly, and motioned for Gorlat to move down the ledge more. He then nodded for the others to climb past him and onto the ledge as well.

He wanted to be first on the bridge. He wanted to take down Picard himself.

Lotre pulled out one of the Federation phasers he'd taken off a stunned crewman and set it to the highest level.

He showed the weapon to the others, then aimed at the door.

"Once in, fan out," he whispered. "Picard is mine."

And he fired a short burst.

The doors decayed outward with an orange flash and a puff of smoke. Balancing on the service rungs, Lotre propelled himself through the hole he'd opened and rolled onto the bridge.

He surged over the guardrail and toward Picard, bringing both the phaser and his own rifle up to aim. His men would take care of any others, and he ignored all but the captain.

Picard's face was etched in surprise as Lotre first backhanded him with his phaser, then dropped the weapon in favor of grabbing Picard's neck and moving him closer.

Blood drizzled from one corner of the Starfleet captain's mouth.

It all felt so good, Lotre thought that perhaps his Klingon blood was betraying his Romulan upbringing.

Should he want this so much, this man's death, that he could taste it? Just for the victory?

No, it wasn't his honor he fought for, it was his master's.

Lotre stabbed the barrel end of his rifle under Picard's chin and didn't stop himself from releasing a tight, dark snigger.

"The *Enterprise*," Lotre whispered mirthfully, "belongs to T'sart."

Look for STAR TREK fiction from Pocket Books

Star Trek®: The Original Series

Star Trek®: New Frontier

Star Trek®: Invasion!

Star Trek®: Day of Honor

#1 • *Ancient Blood* • Diane Carey
#2 • *Armageddon Sky* • L.A. Graf
#3 • *Her Klingon Soul* • Michael Jan Friedman
#4 • *Treaty's Law* • Dean Wesley Smith & Kristine Kathryn Rusch
The Television Episode • Michael Jan Friedman
Day of Honor Omnibus • various

Star Trek®: The Captain's Table

#1 • *War Dragons* • L.A. Graf
#2 • *Dujonian's Hoard* • Michael Jan Friedman
#3 • *The Mist* • Dean Wesley Smith & Kristine Kathryn Rusch
#4 • *Fire Ship* • Diane Carey
#5 • *Once Burned* • Peter David
#6 • *Where Sea Meets Sky* • Jerry Oltion
The Captain's Table Omnibus • various

Star Trek®: The Dominion War

#1 • *Behind Enemy Lines* • John Vornholt
#2 • *Call to Arms...* • Diane Carey
#3 • *Tunnel Through the Stars* • John Vornholt
#4 • *...Sacrifice of Angels* • Diane Carey

Star Trek®: The Badlands

#1 • Susan Wright
#2 • Susan Wright

Star Trek®: Dark Passions

#1 • Susan Wright
#2 • Susan Wright

Star Trek® Books available in Trade Paperback

Omnibus Editions
    Invasion! Omnibus • various
    Day of Honor Omnibus • various
    The Captain's Table Omnibus • various
    Star Trek: Odyssey • William Shatner with Judith and Garfield Reeves-
        Stevens

Other Books

STAR TREK
THE NEXT GENERATION®

TOOTH AND CLAW
Doranna Durgin

While Captain Picard attempts to negotiate a bargain that will save the refugees of a dying planet, Commander Will Riker accompanies a young dignitary to an exclusive hunting preserve. There, technology-damping fields and some of the galaxy's deadliest predators are supposed to test the untried noble's ability in the kaphoora—the hunt. But the shuttlecraft doesn't land on Fandre; it crashes. Riker and the hunting party must fight for their lives with the only weapons they can muster—spears and bat'leth, tooth and claw.

DIPLOMATIC IMPLAUSIBILITY
Keith R.A. De Candido

During the Dominion War, on a conquered world, depleted Klingon forces were overthrown in a small coup d'ètat. The victorious rebels took advantage of the disruption to appeal for recognition from the Federation. Now Klingons have returned to taD and re-established their control of the frozen planet, but the stubborn rebels insist on Federation recognition. A solution to the diplomatic impasse must be found, a task that falls to the Federation's new ambassador to Klingon—Worf.

ON SALE IN FEBRUARY
FROM POCKET BOOKS

DITC

STAR TREK®

STICKER BOOK

MICHAEL OKUDA
DENISE OKUDA
DOUG DREXLER

POCKET BOOKS
A VIACOM COMPANY

STAR TREK

isbn: 0-671-01472-2   STKR

From John Vornholt
author of *Gemworld*

STAR TREK
THE NEXT GENERATION®
THE
GENESIS WAVE
Book Two of Two

Based on the long-hidden scientific secrets of
Dr. Carol Marcus, who has mysteriously
disappeared, the dreaded Genesis Wave is
sweeping across the Alpha Quadrant, transforming
entire planets on a molecular level and threatening
entire civilizations with extinction.

The finest engineers of three civilizations,
including Geordi La Forge and his long-lost love,
Dr. Leah Brahms, must race against time to devise
some way of halting the deadly wave before
yet another world can be transformed into
something entirely alien and unrecognizable.

But even if the Genesis Wave can be defeated,
Picard must still confront the greater mystery of
what unknown intelligence dared to launch the
wave against an unsuspecting galaxy—and for
what malevolent purpose....

Coming in hardcover from

Pocket Books
A VIACOM COMPANY

3086